TAINTED Treats

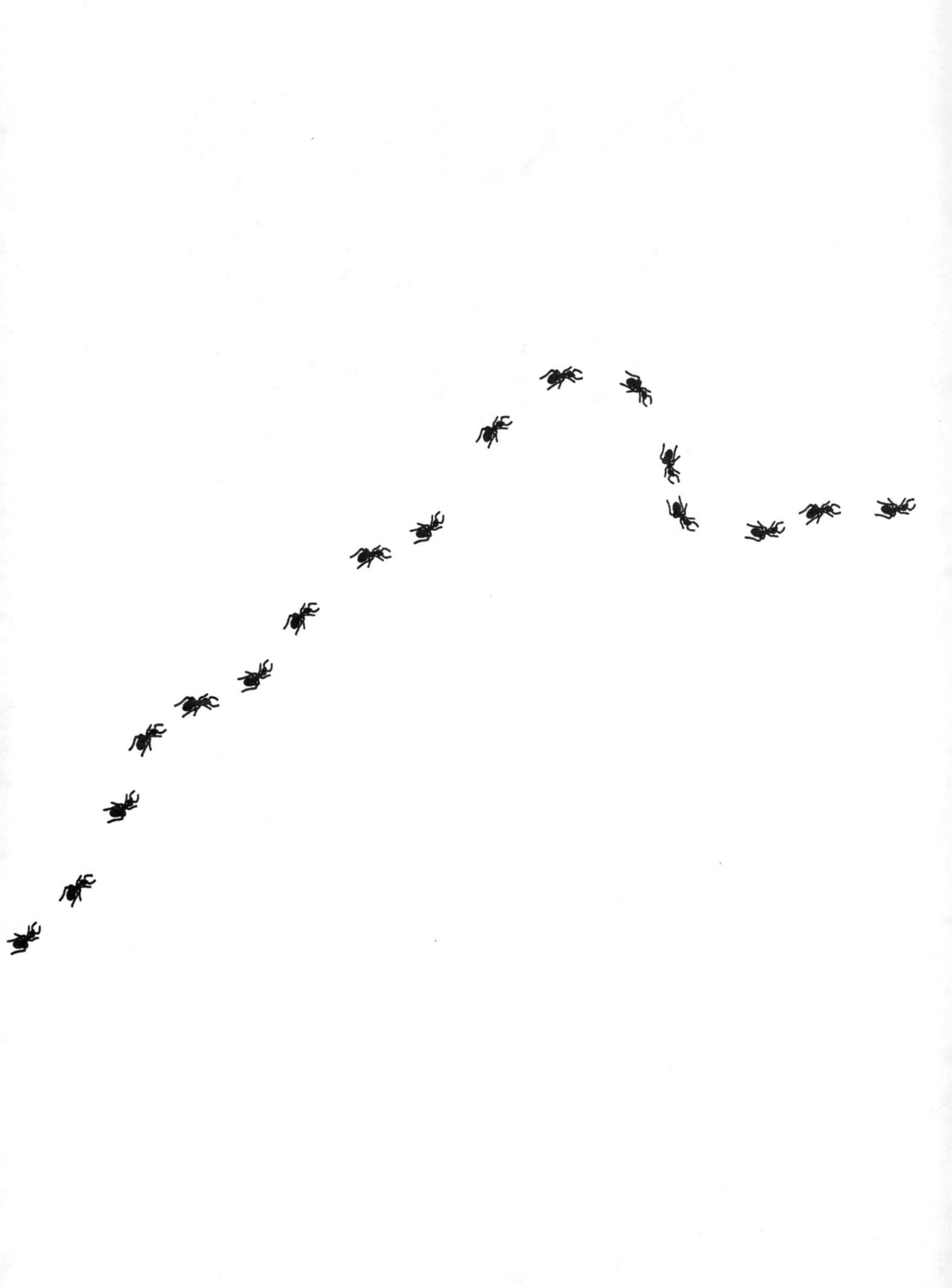

TAINTED *Treats*

R. PAYNE CABEEN

A STREAMLINE PICTURES BOOK

THIS IS A STREAMLINE PICTURES BOOK

Published in the United States by Streamline Pictures, Santa Monica, California.

Publisher's Note: This book is a work of fiction. Names, characters, places, and
incidents are either the product of the author's imagination,
or are used fictitiously, and any resemblance
to actual persons, living or dead, events,
or locales is entirely coincidental.

Cabeen, Robert Payne, IV, 1949-
Tainted Treats. [A collection of horror tales, poems, and drawings, by]
R. Payne Cabeen. [Illustrated by William Stout, Dave Stevens, Simon Bisley,
Mike Mignola, Tim Gula, and R. Payne Cabeen. 1st ed.
Santa Monica, California] Streamline Pictures, 1994.
208 p. illus. 23 cm.

A collection of 5 poems, 3 short stories, and 1 novella
of horror and macabre humor.

1. Horror tales, American. I. Title
PS3561. 813.54

Library of Congress Catalog Card Number: 94-69984.

93021; ISBN: 1-57300-051-5 [limited ed.; $22.95]
93022; ISBN: 1-57300-052-3 [trade ed.; $12.95]

Manufactured in the United States of America

Book & cover design by R. Payne Cabeen

For Albert Feldstein and William M. Gaines,
I am yet another of their mutant spawn,
and to all the artists who
made their stories
scream to life.

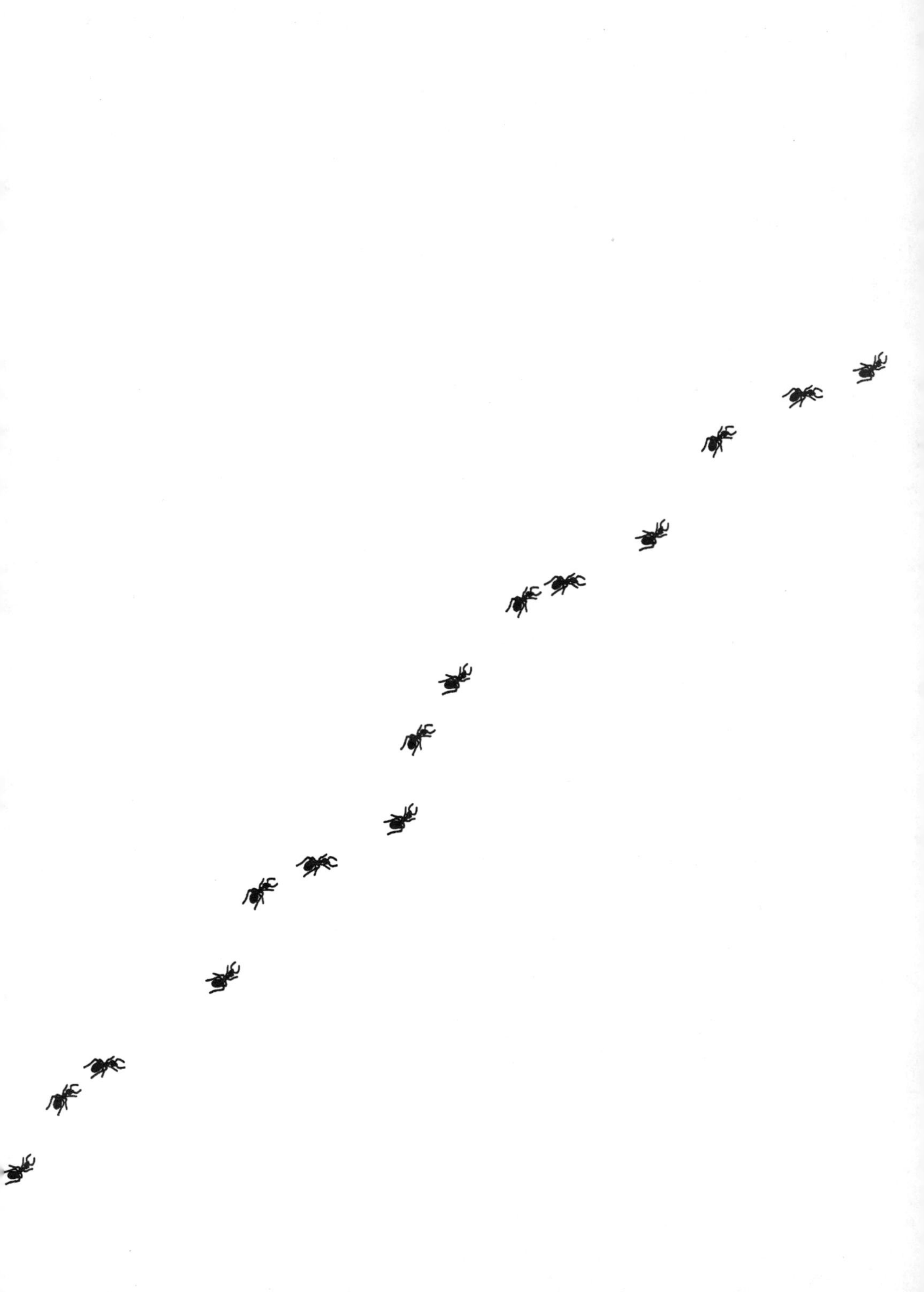

Contents

OSU
NSF
RETRO
ASA
EATON
© 1994 Wm Stout

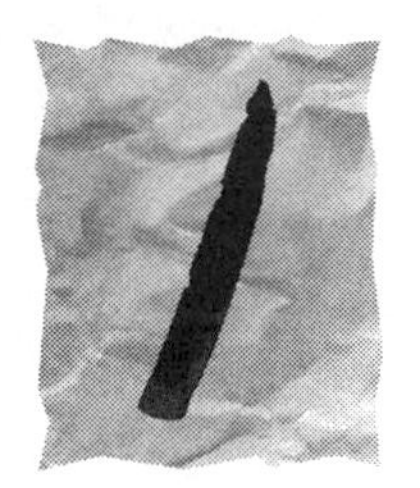

HATE MYSELF

P*AGING Frank Sayer, come to the communication center immediately. Paging Frank Sayer . . .*

A thin, metallic, sing-song voice crackled on a network of cheap army surplus loud speakers. The voice became more and more distorted as it echoed down the narrow institutional halls of Environmental Defense International. It penetrated every square— nonprofit—inch of the sprawling maze of offices that was once a sporting goods warehouse in Trenton, New Jersey. The disembodied pager found its elusive pagee in the shabby EDI cafeteria at the back of the building—next to the copier supply room.

Frank Sayer rooted around his leafy lunch and hoped the disembodied caller would go away. As Director of Field Operations for the world renowned environmental group, he was a veteran of countless bogus emergencies. The middle aged administrator was stocky and energetic. His wiry black hair was just gray enough to give it the appearance of a steel scouring pad. It complemented his abrasive manner perfectly.

He never felt comfortable in adult clothes. Sayer resented the EDI board's mandate that he start dressing his age for the sake of credibility. He also resented the fact that the organization he started in faded *501's* and hiking boots had become a corporation that functioned inside the system. His flesh crawled inside his institutional blue suit. When his name blared a third time, he dropped a fork full of Chinese chicken salad on his recycled paper plate and thrust his arms above his head in unconditional surrender.

He yelled back at the invisible voice, "Okay, okay! I hear you! I can't even eat my damn lunch in peace anymore!"

He buttoned his wrinkled suit coat and began the long walk to the small communications room at the other end of the hall.

Sayer elbowed his way through the doorway and barked, "Okay Collin, this better be good. What have you got?"

The frustrated radio operator pushed his headphones tighter against his ears. He scribbled frantically on a note pad next to his microphone and motioned for everyone to be quiet.

The cramped radio room was packed with an odd assortment of curious EDI staff members. A call was coming in from their Antarctic research team. It was the first communication from the remote science station in a long time. The two quirky scientists hadn't checked in or filed a single report in six months.

The room fell silent as he pleaded with the frantic, distorted voice on the other end of the satellite transmission, "Earthwatch One, do you read me? Earthwatch One! Come in, Earthwatch One!"

Collin threw his head phones down in frustration and yelled, "Damn, I had 'em for a minute, then I lost 'em!"

Frank Sayer was anxious, "Well, did you get anything at all?" Collin picked up the small green pad and replied, "I got something, but it doesn't make any sense."

He ripped the top sheet off the pad and read the cryptic message out loud, "I hate myself . . . I hate myself." The puzzled radio operator waved the note in the air, "That's all, folks."

Sayer grabbed the note from Collin's hand and barked, "What the hell is this supposed to mean?"

Collin shrugged his shoulders, "I don't know. He just kept saying "I hate myself" over and over. It sounded like Ben Eaton to me. He seemed pretty whacked out. He was breathing really heavy and moaning like he was hurt or something."

Sayer shook his head, "I don't like the sound of this. Something's rotten in the ice box and I'm going to wind up eating it before this is over. This whole Antarctic project has been a pain in the ass from the beginning."

A well scrubbed volunteer elbowed her way through the crowd toward Sayer. She was indignant. Her face flushed at her boss's negative comment. It was Neva Dunette, a sharp, attractive graduate student from Columbia University. She looked young for her age, but she was serious and professional. Thick reddish-brown hair framed her tan oval face. Her well defined features were expressive and determined. She was small, physical, spirited and asserted herself when it was necessary. Neva admired Frank Sayer, he was a pioneer in environmental protection, but his flip comments pissed her off. She was a true believer in Earthwatch One. Her enthusiasm for the global pollution monitoring station in Antarctica bordered on fanaticism. She was devoting her entire summer break from Columbia to the well publicized project.

She snapped at Sayer, "Those men are risking their lives to do something really important. You could at least be supportive!"

Sayer remembered what it felt like to feel committed to something. He was one of the first to link CFC's with the depletion of the Earth's ozone layer.

He smiled and lowered his voice, "Chill out, Neva; you've been reading too many of our own press releases. EDI's involved in a lot of important projects. Earthwatch One is just window dressing. Our PR and marketing boys came up with the idea to boost donations and get us on *Nightline.* All the media hype gave the fund raising committee a hard on, and now I'm stuck with it. It's too expensive and too risky."

Neva's voice began to shake, "People have a right to know what's happening to the environment. Eaton and Hardy are gathering critical scientific data down there—information that'll make people want to do something."

Sayer opened a window and pointed outside, "Take a look. You don't have to go to the South Pole to see that we're living in a garbage can. People will do something when they have to wear a body-condom just to walk to the mail box. You don't need a weather man to know which way the wind blows."

A defiant Neva rolled her eyes, "Spare me the Dylan references, Frank. People need hard facts. You just don't give a shit anymore."

Sayer was getting hot, "Let me give you some hard facts. I've got two high-tech prima donnas with three and a half million dollars worth of EDI lab equipment in their hot little hands. They're eleven thousand miles away at the bottom of the damn world, doing God knows what with it. Then, after not hearing from those fucking hot dogs for six months, Eaton gets the urge to reach out and touch someone. So he just calls to let us know that he hates himself. You know their reputation . . . that underwater habitat thing, *Project Pacifica*? The only time the Oceanographic Institute heard from those bastards in eighteen months was when Hardy ran out of his damn chocolate cupcakes. He and *Laurel* only turn on their communication gear when *they* want something. They don't like anyone looking over their shoulder while they work. The way I see it, they're the ones who don't give a shit!"

"What about the radiation readings Hardy found? They were off the scale." Neva rifled through her folder for the figures.

Sayer rubbed his forehead, "That was six months ago. We

asked for more data, but we never heard back from those snowflakes. I don't see why you always make excuses for those idiots. I see you hanging around the communications room waiting for those assholes to report in. You're like a teenager waiting for the phone to ring on a Saturday night."

Neva frowned and snapped, "Somebody around here has to be supportive. How do you know that Eaton and Hardy don't have a perfectly good reason for not calling in?"

"All I know is that those guys are not going to blow this project—not now! I'm probably going to have to go down there and drag their butts back here myself. Since you're so damn interested in this project, I might just drag your supportive ass down there with me."

Neva was quick to take him up on his threat. She grabbed his arm, "Great idea! You won't regret taking me with you, Mr. Sayer. You know me, I'm a team player. I've always wanted to do field work. You can count on me."

Sayer backed up, "Okay, okay, if you're crazy enough to want to freeze your tits off, be my guest. If we haven't gotten through to those pinheads by Friday, we'll leave next week."

Neva beamed, "I'll pack—just in case," and ran back to her office.

Sayer shook his head and crumpled the note. It tumbled from his hand as he slowly walked down the long, cavernous hallway, never noticing that most of the staff had long since vacated the radio room.

Halfway to the cafeteria he yelled back to the radio operator, "Collin, keep trying. And if you get through, tell those jerk-offs that if I have to go down there to drag their asses back here, they'll be digging core samples in Love Canal with their bare hands."

Sayer walked to the cafeteria and plopped down on a beige metal folding chair. He surveyed his droopy salad and jabbed a white plastic fork into a wilted little bale of brownish bean sprouts. He leered down at his room temperature produce, "I hate myself—what kind of message is that?" He vented his frustration on the shriveled salad and chomped away with a vengeance. The staff members and volunteers who crowded the small dining area quietly ate their lunch and tried not to look at him.

Suddenly, Sayer shot out of his chair like a screaming bottle-rocket on the Fourth of July. He knocked over the round institutional table. The half-eaten salad catapulted across the room. An agonizing wail cut through the muffled lunch chatter as he spit out a glob of gruesome greens. The masticated mulch was soaked with blood. It dribbled from his mouth and dripped down his chin. He thrust his tongue out as far as it would go. Everyone in the room gasped. A long, slender, white spike jutted out from the tender tissue on the top of his twitching tongue. It was a prong from his plastic fork. The splintered shard had wedged itself deep in the meaty mass of muscle, veins and nerves. The throbbing wound bled profusely. An amazingly long, slimy drip of blood and saliva spanned the distance between his chin and the dull beige linoleum floor.

Sayer lisped frantically, "Oh thit! Thomebody help me, pleath!"

His pathetic call for help went unanswered. His staff and co-workers just sat there staring at their wounded colleague. If he'd been an aquatic fowl covered with crude oil, they would have come to his assistance immediately. But he wasn't—instead Sayer danced around the room in agony. When it became clear that no one was going to help, he ripped out the jagged spike himself. A fountain of blood spurted from the hideous hole. He screamed. The vascular force of his chronically elevated blood pressure squirted a stream of hot, red fluid on several slow-moving, unsympathetic bystanders at the next table. The rest scrambled for cover as a sticky, scarlet shower of plasma rained down on their food and splattered in their faces.

A well dressed society matron, who volunteered to stuff envelopes twice a week, was overcome by the carnage. She had just finished eating a cucumber, mushroom and guacamole sandwich, a fudge brownie and a pineapple protein smoothy. She wasted no time hurling her entire lunch on the chairman of the fund raising committee. He flicked some of the rancid regurgitation from his stinging eyes and stood motionless with his arms in the air—afraid to touch himself or his surroundings. A scattered pile of white papers on the cluttered tabletop absorbed most of the wet, runny slime. What remained on his neck and chest was a chunky, pungent sludge. Pulpy clumps of pale chartreuse cucumber jutted up like gooey islands in a lumpy lake of frothing phlegm and fudge.

The handsome fund-raiser looked dazed and disoriented as a brown wad of runny mush dripped from his right ear. It must have once been some of the whole wheat bread from her sandwich. Flaccid leaves of oily Romaine lettuce clung to his nose and chin like a hideous second skin. His hair was a matted mass of leafy compost and sour smelling digestive juices. Ironically, a single mushroom had survived its perilous round-trip. The remarkably well-preserved toadstool was welded to his forehead by a gluey glob of partially digested brownie.

Sayer stumbled backwards to the rear wall of the cafeteria as several EDI staffers began to gag uncontrollably. When they witnessed the mortified woman's violent upheaval, they spontaneously blew chow with such force that Sayer had to dodge an airborne volley of vegetables. A vile chain reaction of retching engulfed the room. In a matter of moments, the spotless institutional lunchroom was transformed into a nauseating vomitorium.

A young, athletic, college intern entered the lunchroom unaware. He immediately did a belly-flop in the putrid pond of rising puke and hydroplaned into a group of his fleeing associates. As they flew in all directions and floundered in the sickening slime, Sayer tried to wrap his tongue in an off-white, biodegradable paper napkin. It turned bright red instantly and dissolved within seconds. He sidestepped cautiously across the slippery floor to the cafeteria door, paused at the threshold, looked over his shoulder and lisped, "Thankth a lot ath holeth."

ANTARCTICA, SIX MONTHS EARLIER

A vicious Antarctic wind ripped down the immense south polar ice dome in a murderous frenzy. It slashed across the vast frozen desert like an icy razor. Curtis Hardy turned his huge broad back toward the savage assault. His massive rolls of fat were a constant burden in the warm northern latitudes. But they proved to be a blessing in the frozen wilderness at the bottom of the world. Curtis was more than fat. He was enormous. If he'd been a wrestler instead of a physicist, his name would have been *Humongous* Hardy. This mountain of a man tipped the scales at over four hundred pounds and measured six feet four inches tall in his stocking feet. His extra tonnage was evenly distributed over a massive armature of muscle and bone. Fat was excellent insulation in the freezing polar wind. Unfortunately for Curtis, it never worked that way back home in the land of the weight-conscious.

Hardy was always the one to go out on the ice. His partner, Ben Eaton, couldn't last two minutes in the sixty degree below zero temperature. The wires in his computer had more insulation than he did. Eaton was as skinny as Hardy was fat. His orthodox vegetarian diet was free of fat—and so was he. Everything about him was painfully thin; from his thin red hair to his thin bony toes.

The lab at Earthwatch One was a much more hospitable

working environment. Ben Eaton ran core samples through the mass spectrometer in comfort while Hardy battled the elements alone on the treacherous ice. That wasn't unusual for Curtis Hardy. He'd become accustomed to being left out in the cold—alone with his fat. Hard science was Hardy's vocation, but conducting scientific experiments in Antarctica was harder than he bargained for. He had to work in minus 50° temperatures, dressed in cumbersome clothing, while playing nursemaid to temperamental instruments that got cold and cranky outside the cozy lab. He'd been on the ice for an hour and fifteen minutes, an hour longer than an average person could survive. He was double checking an unusually high radiation reading that he discovered the day before. The radiation specialists back at EDI flipped when they read his report. They wanted more data. The readings seemed to be coming from a cylindrical structure half way between Earthwatch One and an abandoned polar station at McMurdo Sound.

The mysterious black silhouette in the distance looked like trouble. According to the Geiger counter it was definitely hot; the closer he got to the ominous structure, the higher the reading. There was no way to judge its exact size or distance. His field glasses were useless. They fogged up when they got anywhere near his hot face. The suspicious shape seemed to hover in the seamless expanse of white-on-white. The ice was white. The sky was white. Everything was white except the mysterious black shape and the red warning light on his Geiger counter. It flashed like a cop car on a Saturday night. Hardy stopped. Then a light flashed in Hardy's suspicious brain. The damn thing was probably one of those portable nuclear reactors that were popular with the super-powers in the early sixties. There must have been a horrible accident or a meltdown to account for the unbelievably high radiation readings.

Hardy crammed his fat ass in the cluttered cab of his lumbering, rusted-out Spryte. The mammoth snow vehicle

coughed and belched noxious fumes as its tired engine gasped for air. The worn-out mountain of machinery groaned and lurched toward Earthwatch One. Hardy couldn't wait to tell Eaton about the nuke and eat lunch—or was it dinner time. Actually it may have been breakfast. He never knew for sure anymore. It was summer in Antarctica. Since the Vernal Equinox it was sunny twenty-four hours a day. Never warm, just sunny.

His lethargic Spryte rumbled slowly across the mile deep ice sheet. A vile petroleum stench permeated the uncomfortable cabin, but at least it was dry and warm. Curtis could almost taste the cream filled chocolate cupcakes that waited for him back at the lab. There were a dozen cases of them left in the store room. When they ran out—he ran out. After twenty minutes of treading ice, he was almost home. Earthwatch One wasn't much to look at. But it looked like home in the middle of the desolate Antarctic desert. Especially since it was the only thing visible in the lifeless, white wasteland.

As he neared his prefabricated habitat, he saw an unfamiliar snow vehicle heading straight for him. Its high-pitched whine, sounding like a powerful jet engine, echoed in the distance. Whatever it was—was moving fast. It screamed toward him with a blue flame shooting out the back. A plume of crushed ice fanned out behind it twenty feet in the air. When it was almost on top of him, it slowed down and skidded sideways to a stop. Two uniformed men jumped out. In Antarctica, any time two guys wore the same color Goretex parka—it was a uniform. Curtis waved—they didn't.

The next thing he knew, he was eating glass. A volley of bullets ripped through the windshield of his Spryte. He dove for the floor, but didn't make it that far. He only managed to wedge himself between the dash and the seat, so he ducked his head and covered his eyes. It was enough. He heard more gunfire—machine-gun fire—and lots of it. The matched pair

played a nine millimeter duet on their Uzis—vivo fortissimo. Curtis didn't like the tune. It was too fast and too loud. He covered his ears and waited for their performance to be over. The deadly duo played everything they knew, then packed up and went home.

Curtis squeezed back in his seat and peered out the shattered rear window. The mysterious snow-Ferrari was almost out of sight. It raced toward McMurdo Sound. He'd never seen anything move that fast through the ice and snow. It certainly wasn't an EDI vehicle. It was much too high performance for any foundation budget. It was definitely government issue. But which government? There were plenty of frozen flags buried beneath the unforgiving ice to choose from.

The wind changed direction. A strong odor of gasoline and kerosene seared his nostrils and stung his eyes—MO-GAS! He tried to open the bullet riddled door. The lock was jammed. He tried the other—jammed. Curtis dove for the empty windshield frame. It was big and wide. He was bigger and wider. His enormous belly wedged tight halfway through the unyielding steel frame. Luckily, his legs were long and incredibly strong from dragging around all his excess baggage. He planted his feet on either side of the rear window and pushed as hard as he could.

The desperate physicist applied several laws of physics simultaneously and popped through the opening. The sudden expenditure of kinetic energy gave him tremendous forward momentum. He sailed across the hood of the Spryte and became airborne. After a dozen or so feet of low earth orbit, gravity prevailed and his tremendous belly touched down on the ice with a dull splat.

The sudden impact forced the air from his lungs, but didn't slow him down much. He slid like a huge hockey puck for another twenty feet, spun around a few times and came to a stop. His arms and legs spread out in all directions. He gasped for breath and pushed himself up on his hands and knees.

Struggling to his feet, Hardy looked back at his bullet-ridden vehicle with a puzzled and indignant expression on his face—(the way people look down at the sidewalk after they trip.) A widening pool of mo-gas spread out under the wounded steel behemoth. Then . . . it blew up. Not all at once—first it burst into flames. Then a red and yellow fire ball erupted from the fuels-tank and lifted the scorched, sheet-metal skinned beast several feet in the air. A thunderous blast spun Curtis around as the iron chassis of the mindless brute spewed its mechanical guts. Thick black smoke billowed from every ruptured orifice. The doors blew out the sides and the hood blew straight up. The explosion was slow—like in the movies. Either his brain was working faster or time had slowed down. It seemed to take forever for the hood to stop spinning in the air and return to earth. When it finally did, it landed upright in a drift of snow like a bright orange sheet-metal tombstone. Curtis stood there dazed. His arms hung limp at his sides. The oily, ebony smoke scribbled meaningless graffiti across the cold white sky. Curtis was just beginning to comprehend what had happened, when another explosion rocked him from behind.

This one didn't happen slowly. It was fast and loud and bigger—much bigger. When he whipped around, the concussion knocked the wind out of him like a sucker punch to the gut. He gasped a breathless "NO!" The wind blew the word back in his face. In a heartbeat, debris from Earthwatch One rained down on him. There was no fire—just smoke. The force of the explosion snuffed out the flames at the moment of combustion. All that remained of the compound was smoking rubble.

Curtis threw the full weight of his massive body at the glacial wall of wind and plodded toward the smoldering wreckage. Each breath stabbed his lungs like a frozen knife.

Many had perished on the ice only a few feet from food and shelter. It took all his strength to lift his huge legs. But his throbbing pillars of bone and meat slowly closed the gap one agonizing step at a time.

When he reached the devastated compound he was exhausted. Earthwatch One was a tangled maze of twisted metal and expensive junk. An electron microscope hung, intact, from a jumble of wires and crumpled metal shelving. It looked like a high-tech spider in a web of trashed technology. The lab was completely destroyed. The store room's roof, and one wall, had completely blown away. Most of the food supplies had been incinerated. Charred provisions and shattered equipment littered the ice for fifty yards around the demolished science station.

Curtis surveyed the damage in disbelief. The condition of the living quarters would determine his chances for survival. If they were intact, he would live. If they were damaged, even slightly, he would die. They were below the surface of the ice, so there was a chance they had survived the blast. He stumbled to the narrow, crudely chiseled stairs and descended ten feet in the ancient ice. Curtis lifted a mangled storage drum out of the icy stairwell and discovered that the living quarters were still intact. He pulled the heavy insulated door open. It was dark and smokey inside. Ben Eaton was coughing in the corner. The explosion had rearranged the furniture. Curtis cleared a haphazard path through the obstacle course of personal belongings to his friend. Ben was dazed, but he was still in one piece. Curtis lifted his light, wiry body and gently lowered him onto a wood and canvas chair.

Curtis threw back the hood of his parka, "Are you all right? Everything on the surface is trashed!"

Ben nodded then mumbled, "What the fuck happened up there?"

Curtis told him what little he knew, then made his way to

the door, "I'm going top-side to see what I can salvage. Take it easy Ben. I'll try to turn the juice back on."

Curtis squeezed his partner's shoulder for reassurance and went outside. He checked the generator. It was in good shape. After a few minutes of minor tinkering, the power came back on. Fortunately, the huge fuel tanks were buried deep beneath the ice and survived the blast. The situation at Earthwatch One looked a little better. Curtis rummaged through the store room for food and medical supplies. He was relieved to find seventeen boxes of food that were still intact. Unfortunately, they were all dehydrated tofu. The gastronomic ramifications of his grim discovery were devastating to the junk-food epicurean. He whimpered and continued searching the wreckage. After poking around the debris for half an hour, he found what was left of a radio. Then something caught his eye. Behind a shattered computer monitor, something shiny and brown glinted in the harsh polar sunlight. His heart raced. Could it possibly be . . . ? It was. Curtis lunged at the monitor and pushed it aside. A twin pack of cream filled chocolate cupcakes was nestled in a drift of smoking debris. Curtis lifted his treasure to his frostbitten lips, blew the dust off and kissed it. He looked up into the stark white sky and cried, "Thank you, Lord!" He slipped them in his pocket and hauled the salvaged goods back to the sleeping quarters.

Ben had recovered enough to straighten the tiny room. He helped Curtis with the boxes and together they pushed the thick metal door closed behind them. Ben took a quick mental inventory of the supplies and sighed with relief.

He broke open the boxes of food one by one and squealed in delight, "Look at this, TOFU! We have enough high quality vegetable protein to last for months."

Curtis muttered sarcastically, "Yea, that's great, Ben. I've always wanted to go on a bean curd and water diet."

Ben rubbed his hands together gleefully and said, "Come

on, Curtis, it'll be good for you. You'll be eating healthy for a change. Relax, I'll make dinner. Besides, you can afford to lose a few lousy pounds."

Curtis smirked and replied, "I could lose a few lousy pounds if I threw your bony ass outside. No tofu for me tonight, thanks." He removed the cupcakes from his pocket with a flourish, sniffed them and sighed, "Ah, sweet ambrosia!"

Ben moaned, "I can't believe you. Those things are full of empty calories and preservatives."

"They just may preserve my sanity while I watch you eat that pasty bean slime." Curtis peeled back the clear plastic wrapper and removed a moist cupcake.

Ben boiled some water on the hot plate and added a handful of small white cubes. Curtis waited politely while Ben poured bubbling water in a coffee cup and plopped the quivering gelatinous blobs on a small plate.

Curtis said, "You're not going to drink that scummy water you cooked that slop in, are you?"

Ben was indignant, "I certainly am. The water contains vital nutrients that were lost when I cooked the tofu."

Then he took a sip of the hot cloudy water. Curtis winced and turned his attention to the deep brown object of his desire. As an appetizer, he licked off the white frosting squiggle that rested gently on a smooth layer of velvety fudge. Below, the dark moist cake yielded to his ardent advances. Then suddenly, it revealed the sweet, creamy secrets of its soft, hidden center. An explosion of delicate flavors and subtle textures rewarded the tip of his eager tongue. One greedy bite led to another until the first precious cupcake had vanished. He ravaged the last cupcake in a frenzy of chocolate lust. Ben quietly slurped his steaming tofu like a pious monk.

Ben broke the silence, "Are any of the other science stations close enough to walk to?"

Curtis licked the two circular chocolate remnants on the

slick white cardboard packaging and said, "No."

"I didn't think so," Ben stared into the milky residue on his empty plate.

Curtis mindlessly folded the crinkly, clear plastic cupcake wrapper, "We're safe right where we are for now. I just hope those guys I ran into out on the ice don't pay us another surprise visit. Whoever's signing their paychecks had a nuke go critical and now they want to keep it quiet. If we don't lie low, we'll wind up sleeping with the penguins."

Ben nodded adding, "Guess we'll just have to sit this one out here till EDI comes looking for us. I'll try to get them on the radio." He fiddled with the broken jumble of wires and circuits for over an hour. "We definitely can't receive, but I'm pretty sure we can send. There's no way to tell for sure if we're getting through."

After trying to send a message for several hours they fell asleep. Their quarters were heated, but it was still painfully cold. Their fur parkas and insulated pants kept them from freezing. The two marooned scientists slept long, but not very well. Curtis thrashed around and dreamed of food. Two cupcakes weren't even a snack for him. His usual fare consisted of: two medium rare steaks, a whole fried chicken, several baked potatoes, a loaf of white bread with real butter, half a dozen cream filled chocolate cupcakes, or a whole Boston cream pie, and a six-pack of diet cola.

Curtis woke up hungry. Not toast and orange juice hungry—mean hungry. After all, he was eating for two—himself and the two hundred pounds of fat that lived inside him. While Ben slept, he went out on the ice and searched the compound for any remnant from his provisions. He sifted through the rubble and turned over every piece of debris—nothing—not even a crumb. There was a gnawing ache in his stomach that was unlike anything he felt before. In the back of his mind, he always thought that the reason he ate so much

was that he was hungry. But the desperate emptiness he now felt was different. It actually hurt. Less than twenty-four hours had passed since he gorged himself last. He knew the pain was only going to get worse. When he returned, he was nearly in a panic. Ben made it worse.

He said, "Hey Curtis, look at this!" and switched on the small color TV with a cordless remote, "The satellite dish is still working." He roamed aimlessly through the channels.

Curtis yelled, "Stop! Hold it right there, damn it!"

A cooking segment on a morning talk show was in progress. The tiny screen was filled with a tender wedge of browned beef fillet. It ascended slowly from a deep iron pot filled with boiling butter. The tempting tidbit sizzled on a long silver fork.

"Do you know what that is?" Curtis moaned in delight and anguish.

The vigilant vegetarian sneered and answered, "Yea, that looks like dead animal flesh impaled on a sharp metal skewer. It seems to have been boiled in what appears to be pure cholesterol."

The crazed omnivore ignored his friend and answered his own question, "That's Boeuf Fondu Bourguignonne, my friend. That's real food you're looking at there."

"All I see is a heart attack on a stick." Ben started boiling water to rehydrate his tofu breakfast. "When you eat meat, you're eating pure death. The fear the cow felt when it was slaughtered winds up in the meat. It's full of adrenaline. They pump the animal full of steroids, antibiotics, appetite stimulants and whatever else they can think of to increase their profits."

Curtis wasn't listening. He sat mesmerized as the lovely actress/model who hosted the show raised the delectable morsel to her lips. She crooned, "Oh, it smells *sooo* good," as she puckered and blew on the steaming fillet.

Curtis egged her on, "Go ahead, baby. Do it. Pop the whole

thing in your mouth. Open up. Don't tease me. Do it now!"

The willowy blond cocked her head, lowered the fork and coyly said, "I really shouldn't. I have to watch my figure—or no one else will." The audience laughed. "Maybe our weatherman could help me out here." More laughs. The camera cut to the big friendly guy. He shook his head and patted his bulging belly. The audience was in stitches.

"Why do people on TV always pretend like they never eat anything," Curtis whined in frustration.

The chef looked like a French race car driver in a tall white hat. He said, "No, no, no, mademoiselle. You must taste eet. Jus one leetle bite."

By the sound of their applause, it was obvious that the audience agreed with the handsome cook.

Curtis scooted closer to the screen. His enthusiasm had returned, "That's right, buddy, make her eat it!"

She glanced shyly off camera, took the tiniest bird-bite imaginable and exclaimed, as if her mouth was actually full, "Ummm, that's de—licious!"

Curtis jumped to his feet—insane with hunger. He clawed at the fat on his gnawing gut and roared, "You anorexic bitch, eat the fucking meat! They're only paying you two million dollars a year to do this shit. You could at least eat the fucking meat!"

Ben quickly grabbed the remote from Curtis' hand. Click—cartoons—a cat chased a canary with a meat cleaver. Click—a commercial—golden brown fried chicken in a bucket. Click, click, click—the medical channel—close-ups of a gall bladder operation.

He left it there and shook Curtis, "Snap out of it! It's not like we don't have any food. You'll feel much better after you've eaten some nice warm tofu."

Ben dipped a large aluminum spoon into the pot of boiling soy-sludge and scooped out several plump, soggy white cubes. He plopped them down on a plate and handed them to Curtis, who whimpered and stared at them in horror as the limp lumps quivered in a pool of hot milky water. The hollow stabbing pain in the center of his stomach was unbearable. The Boeuf Fondu Bourguignonne on TV had only intensified his urge to sink his teeth into something firm and meaty. A seething stew of digestive juices percolated in his gurgling gut. In desperation, he picked up one of the wretched things and took a bite. It didn't taste bad. In fact, it didn't taste like anything at all. But the consistency was awful. A shiver went down his spine as the slimy paste mushed around in his mouth. He closed his eyes and swallowed. He shuddered as the slippery lump slithered down his throat. Then mercifully, it was gone. He decided that it would be less disgusting if he swallowed them whole. So he gulped the horrible cubes down one by one. In a matter of moments it was over. The pain in his stomach began to ease, then disappeared. His hunger had subsided, but he was far from satisfied.

Ben kept his mouth shut. But when he saw the bilious expression on his friend's face, he couldn't stifle a laugh. It came out as a wheezy, high-pitched squeal.

Curtis went into orbit, "You self-satisfied son of a bitch! I'd like to see the look on your face if my chocolate cupcakes and frozen steaks were the only food that survived the blast."

He threw a pillow at his friend so hard that it knocked him on his butt. They both laughed hysterically. Ben stuck the pillow under his shirt and did an impersonation of Curtis eating tofu. They laughed until it hurt.

Ben put his head between his knees and tried to catch his breath, "Let's watch some TV."

They watched a game show, an old episode of *Leave it to Beaver*, some rock videos and a couple of hours of assorted soap operas. Then it was time for lunch. Ben cooked the tofu and Curtis ate it. This time the quivering cubes went down a little easier. After lunch—more TV. They watched a real life courtroom drama, an early black and white episode of *Gilligan's Island*, and a glitzy game show. The tofu went down easier still—then more TV. They flipped around between three afternoon talk shows and speculated if the guests were ringers. They decided that it didn't really matter because the shows were just a chatty form of wrestling. The topic that held their interest was *Frigid Men and the Women Who Love Them*. After that, they caught the last few minutes of a beach volleyball championship on the sports channel. Then it was time for dinner—more tofu—more TV. They stopped on a premium channel halfway through the remake of *The Thing*. The movie made them both nervous so they switched to the religious channel and watched a hypnotic preacher with a beard show home movies while he smoked a cigar. When they got tired of that, they turned to a comedy club show, then a public television pledge break, then the all news channel until they slipped into unconsciousness.

The next few days were the same as the first, tofu, TV, tofu, TV, tofu—then more TV. As the days passed, Curtis found it easier to eat the sordid soybean curds. They were still revolting, but he just didn't care about food much anymore. By the sixth week he didn't care about food at all. He ate to live—nothing more. Eventually even the doughnut commercials didn't make him hungry.

The nonstop television routine added a strange structure to their monotonous existence. It became their job—their reason for being. The days passed so quickly that they couldn't find time to radio for help more than once or twice a month. The television even provided them with romance. Curtis had a crush on a shapely female body builder who came on the sports channel every morning. She was big and blond and beautiful. Her tan body rippled with muscles in all the right places.

Whenever she bent over to pick up her free weights Curtis would pant, "Look at those glutes, Ben. I'm in love. You're looking at the mother of my children."

He even went so far as to join in during the aerobic exercises. After awhile, Curtis' body began to change. He was actually beginning to lose some weight. He was still big, but he lost at least a hundred pounds by the third month.

Once during a particularly strenuous workout, Curtis' girlfriend worked up a healthy sweat. Her tan, athletic body glistened in the mottled sunshine that filtered through the lush tropical palm trees in her warm, exotic exercise venue. Wet Lycra and firm young flesh was too much for Ben.

Curtis caught him whacking-off in the corner. Curtis was furious, "She's mine, you pervert. She'd never fall for a skinny weasel like you!"

"Take it easy, I was looking at her assistant," Ben sheepishly stopped pounding his pecker and zipped his pants.

"You better not get any ideas!" Curtis changed the channel just in case.

After dinner, Ben had a standing date with a newswoman. She recapped the major events of the day every thirty minutes. Curtis couldn't see the attraction. She was a handsome, authoritative woman, with curly hair that changed color every few weeks. But she certainly didn't warrant the sad puppy whimpers and obsessive attention that Ben lavished on her.

One night Curtis just came right out and asked, " I don't get it, Ben. With all the beautiful women on television—why her?

"Why her? I'll tell you why her! Look at those lips."

"What about them? They look like ordinary lips to me."

"Those are no ordinary lips! Are you blind? See how full and pouty they are? Each word they speak is a kiss."

Curtis was sorry he asked.

Ben jumped up and yelled, "Did you see that?" He

moaned, "Ooooh, just look at that," and slapped his cheeks.

"I didn't see anything."

"Watch closely. There! Right there!"

Curtis did see something, but it was subtle. At the end of each sentence, the corner of her mouth turned up ever so slightly. It was a cross between a cynical sneer and a faint smile.

The crotch of Ben's pants bulged skyward like a pup tent.

He leered at the TV and sighed, "She drives me wild when she does that thing with her mouth." He started to sweat, "She knows more than she's telling, Curtis. She knows everything. All about me and the way I feel about her. She's looking at me right now." Ben pulled his pants down and began to twitch. "She likes what she sees, Curtis. Look at her. She's smiling at me."

Ben started to shake. A telephone company commercial came on and he collapsed into a blubbering pile of frustration. His right leg twitched and thumped out a series of staccato beats. Perhaps it was a strange mating signal that only his satellite news-goddess could understand. Or maybe Ben was one news break over the line.

Curtis helped him to his cot, pulled a heavy wool blanket over him and whispered, "That's enough TV for you, little man. Tomorrow's another day."

Curtis found the remote and did something he hadn't done in a long time. He turned the TV off! Then he eased onto his cot, folded his arms tight against his chest and stared at the ceiling. The slumber party was over. He could feel it in his bones. The room seemed suddenly small. The TV had been on twenty-four hours a day for over four months. When he turned the damn thing off, it was as if he'd bricked up his only window on the outside world. The room was only nine feet wide by twelve feet long. But now it felt smaller—much smaller—more like a prefabricated coffin with all the amenities. He became aware of his breathing. The air felt thick

and heavy. It pressed down on his chest. He couldn't take a deep breath, so he bit off small bite-sized chunks of air and gulped them into his gasping lungs.

Then he felt it—the silence. He never noticed it before. Now, he couldn't imagine how something so monstrous could have stayed hidden for so long? The dense invisible force made him feel numb and hollow. A mindless, absorbent stillness enveloped the room. It sucked the sound out of his ears. Not even an empty echo remained. The silence had been there all along—waiting—patient. The way death waits patiently for that one little slip-up, that one wrong turn—that one last heart beat.

Curtis wanted to scream, but he was afraid. What if he screamed and no sound came out? What if the silence ripped the scream from his throat and devoured it before it reached his ears? His hands felt inert. When he tried move his fingers, they felt like they belonged to someone else—someone dead. The lights began to flicker off. Once, twice—then total darkness. Curtis stiffened in terror. The hungry void that surrounded him swallowed the sum total of all that he was. The room, his body, Ben—everything vanished in its vast empty belly. It felt like the lid to his coffin had slammed shut. Only his thoughts remained, and they were even darker than the nothingness that consumed him. A suffocating panic squeezed him from all directions. An ominous sense of spiritual dread slashed him like the savage polar wind. It was cold and silent and dead. The force of its frozen darkness blew out the gentle flame that burned in the center of his being. Everything that was bright and warm was gone. All that remained was the cold, silent darkness—and the fear.

He lay paralyzed for an eternity of heartbeats. Curtis had never been afraid of the dark, or even death. The terror he felt went far beyond the fear of simple oblivion. He sensed that if he froze in this barren wasteland at the bottom of the world, he might have to endure a conscious awareness of the unyielding silence for a billion years. Or at least until the ice melted. He had only experienced the ghastly void for a few minutes and it was already unbearable. He envied the dead in their lush green cemeteries. At least their bones enjoyed the attention of worms. No life form of any kind would assist in his decomposition. He'd simply freeze solid in the sterile ice and remain unchanged until the sun went super nova and incinerated the entire solar system. Curtis couldn't wait that long to be warm again. Something tepid and wet slowly crept down his temple. Then he heard a tiny sound. It was the faint drum beat of a single tear dropping on his taught canvas cot. Nothing ever sounded so sweet. The lights flickered on. Once, twice—then a harsh fluorescent glare filled the room.

Curtis knew exactly what he had to do. There was only one thing noisy enough keep the silence away for good. He moved one leg, then the other. The dense compression of the room made it almost impossible for him to continue. He inched his way to the remote in the middle of the floor and clicked it on. A tiny white speck in the center of the TV screen exploded into a cheerful rectangle of vivid color. Crackling fragments of sound raced through a maze of circuits to catch up with the with the emerging picture. *Zap*—the shopping channel filled the flickering screen.

A little boy ran through a meadow of tall grass and wild flowers. He was only painted glaze on a porcelain collector's plate, but he had everything Curtis wanted. He wore tattered overalls with paisley patches, a blue and yellow striped shirt and black high-top sneakers. A gentle summer breeze tossed his sandy blond hair as he flew a bright red kite. A golden eagle was stenciled across the taught tissue paper. The kite's long, knotted, dishrag tail curved lazily in a water color sky. Comfy white clouds drifted slowly in the warm, clean air. Curtis could breathe again. The silence retreated to its hiding

place. Everything was the same as before. Except for one thing—now he knew what would happen if he ever turned the TV *off* again.

A melodic feminine voice described the limited edition plate in amazing detail. The camera zoomed in to capture every cheerful brushstroke. It seemed impossible that anyone could have so much to say about anything. Curtis didn't mind. He would have gladly ordered a plate if he had a phone. The orders rolled in and the voice droned on. Curtis fell asleep. He dreamed of warm, lazy afternoons and soaring kites. But somewhere beyond the wild flower meadows, the hideous silence waited for him to turn off the TV.

At six a.m. a fast talking pitch-man started hawking a fake diamond ring. Curtis opened his eyes and watched the cubic zirconium bauble slowly rotate on its clear Lucite base. He felt cold. He hadn't shaken the icy feeling of dread that crept into his bones the night before. Ben had been awake for quite awhile. He silently boiled a pot of water as Curtis stretched and walked toward him. Ben seemed detached as he stared down at the rolling bubbles.

Curtis broke the silence, "Well, what's for breakfast today?"

"We're not having breakfast today, or lunch, or dinner." Ben didn't laugh or even smile. "There's no more tofu, Curtis. We ate the last of it for dinner."

"What? Why didn't you tell me we were running low?"

"What good would that have done?"

"We could have rationed it out or something."

"It doesn't matter. Nobody's coming for us. Haven't you figured that out yet? We've been here for four and a half months."

Curtis ran to the boxes to see for himself. They were empty. Not even one crumbly curd was left.

Ben handed him a cup of plain boiled water, "Sip this. It might help. Have you ever gone on a fast?"

"No. Have you?"

“Yea, lots of times.”

“How long?”

“Usually a day or two. One time I fasted for two weeks. It was very purifying.”

“You’re so skinny I don’t see how you could go that long.”

“I got pretty weak toward the end, but I felt really good. It cleaned my whole system out. You just have to drink a lot of water and take it easy.”

“How long do you think we can last?”

Ben set his cup down and looked at the ceiling, “I can’t say for sure. I don’t have much body fat. I could last a month, maybe more. You’ve still got a lot of fat left, you’ll last much longer. At least until the fat’s all gone.”

Curtis channel-surfed mindlessly. He didn’t watch anything, he just zapped one show after another. He went right past his girlfriend without even saying hello. The idea of not having anything to eat didn’t bother him. He lost the desire for food months ago. It was the idea of slow death that made him feel numb. Knowing was the hard part. Knowing that life would slip away, little by little, day by day. Knowing that Ben would starve first and he’d have to watch. Knowing that he’d be alone when the silence came back for him—this time for good. He flipped through the channels faster and pressed the button harder as if somehow the remote could change his fate.

After several hours of zombie-zapping, Ben took the remote away from Curtis and flipped to a soap opera. Eventually Curtis got back into the routine and the hours passed quickly until they both fell asleep. The next day started off as usual, but in the middle of *Gilligan’s Island*, Curtis started feeling strange. A monkey in a spacesuit landed on the island in an old Mercury capsule. The precocious primate thought Gilligan was his mother. Everyone was kissing the chimp’s ass because he was the the only one who knew which button turned on the rescue beacon in the antique spacecraft.

The Professor made a baby bottle out of bamboo and filled it with coconut milk. At the point where Mr. and Mrs. Howell insisted that they were the monkey's grandparents, Curtis broke out in a cold sweat.

He was ashen and started to shake, "Ben, my head feels like it's going to burst."

"That's normal. It's just the poisons flushing out of your system."

"What poisons?"

"All the poisons that you've worked so hard to accumulate over the years. With what you eat, there must be a toxic waste dump inside your body. The pesticides, preservatives and pollution collect in your fat. The fast is flushing them out. They're just taking one last crack at you on the way out. Drink more water. It'll only last for a couple of days."

Curtis crawled to his cot and stayed there for almost two weeks. Ben brought him water every hour. He was too weak to make it to the chemical toilet so he pissed in a bottle. The first few days, he vomited green mucus and blew slimy yellow diarrhea out his ass. When that stopped, he just drifted in and out of sleep for days at a time. He finally opened his eyes on the twelfth day and he felt great. His body felt different. The weakness had passed. Now he felt strong and centered. A warm glow burned in the center of his belly. It replaced any feeling of emptiness. His heart beat slow and strong. His whole body buzzed with a tingling energy. A profound feeling of lightness lifted his spirits. He never felt better in his entire life. His brain was clear, his thoughts were positive. He was confident and serene.

Curtis bounded out of bed to tell Ben the good news. Ben was still asleep. His breathing was shallow and labored. Ben didn't look so good. He'd always been skinny, but in a healthy way. Now he just looked frail. He lay there with his mouth gaping open. His teeth and tongue were dry and his breath

smelled like rotten fish. It was easy to imagine the way he'd look when he was dead.

Curtis had to do something with all the energy that was bottled up inside him. He stripped down to his shorts and started doing pushups. He'd never done them before. After fifty or sixty, the muscles in his arms and chest burned. It felt good. He did some sit-ups, then every exercise he could remember from his girlfriend's show. The harder he worked-out, the better he felt. Curtis took a deep breath. Sweat poured off him and he was breathing hard, but he wasn't tired.

When Ben finally got out of bed, he sighed, "I can see you're feeling better today."

"Never better!" Curtis grabbed a towel and rubbed it hard all over his body. "This fasting business is great. If I'd known it would make me feel like this, I'd have done it a long time ago."

Ben tried to laugh, but coughed instead. "I'm glad you feel so good. I feel lousy."

"You're just going through what I went through. You'll feel great any day now."

"I hope so, but I doubt it. I've been on a lot of fasts, but I've never felt like this before. You're body is burning fat. I'm burning up muscle and organ tissue."

Ben didn't start to feel better. He just got worse. After three weeks without food, his health had deteriorated to a shocking degree. His pale, transparent skin had a sickening amber cast. It showed everything below its thin, waxy surface. Veins, gristle, bones, and what little muscle remained were all too easy to see. Ben looked like a hideous see-through man—a walking anatomy lesson. It hurt Curtis to look at him when he gave him his sponge-bath.

Ben's pelvis jutted out from all sides like a grotesque, bony fin. It was covered with small raw ulcers where his paper thin skin had been rubbed away by his clothing and bed linen. Every angle and convolution on his spine was visible. Where his back bowed in the middle, the sharp vertebra had erupted through his skin. Dry white bone peeked through angry red openings that had scabbed over countless times. The slightest movement was painful, but Ben still managed to get around. When he shuffled to the bathroom, Curtis had to look away.

Curtis felt frustrated and guilty. His physical condition improved every day. He tried to help Ben, but there wasn't much he could do. He let him control the remote and went along with whatever he wanted to watch. Sometimes Ben barely had enough strength to push the buttons. As they watched a dog show on the sports channel, Ben picked his scabs. A commercial came on that had a strange effect on Ben. It was a 30 second spot for a chain of western-style steak houses. An extreme close-up of a knife sliced through a two inch slab of rare red meat. Hot bloody juice oozed from the fleshy slit.

Ben sprang to life and cried, "That's what I want! Meat! Any kind of meat, as long as it's hot and bloody!"

Curtis was shocked, "That's a switch. It was actually grossing me out. I thought all you ate was rabbit food?"

"I haven't eaten meat in fifteen years, but I want it now."

Blood-lust was in Ben's eyes. He rubbed his thighs and rocked back and forth as he sobbed, "I want to live, Curtis. There's a lot of things I haven't done. I want to own a convertible. I want to get married and have kids. I've spent most of my adult life trying to save the environment. I want to live in a wonderful world like that Louis Armstrong song. I haven't done anything for myself. I deserve something, don't I? All I want is a piece of meat. Just one piece of bloody—fucking—meat!"

Curtis sat next to Ben and tried to calm him down, "I'll get you some meat. We'll be rescued soon. I'll take you to one of those steak houses. We'll eat steaks till we shit hamburgers. You'll see."

Then Curtis flopped down on his cot and watched the prize-winning dogs prance and pose for the judges until he nodded off and slipped into a vivid dream. He became one of the judges at the dog show. As he bent over to put a blue ribbon on a frisky wire-haired terrier, the docile show dog turned rabid. In a heartbeat the well behaved canine turned into a snarling ball of bristling fur and snapping jaws. It lunged and sunk its frothing, razor sharp teeth deep into the delicate architecture of his bare throat. Curtis felt the cartilage in his larynx shatter as the maniacally yipping little beast ripped it out. The savage terrier quickly ran away with his gory prize. Curtis chased the agile creature around the sprawling arena, but he couldn't run fast enough. When he tried to yell for the dog to stop, hot, moist air whistled and wheezed through the gaping hole in his throat, but no sound came out. There was no pain and no blood, just a ragged void surrounded by shredded flesh, tendons and dry rubbery veins. As Curtis probed the meaty cavern with his trembling fingertips, the dream evaporated into warm, black nothingness and he descended into a deep dreamless sleep.

The television flickered like an electric campfire. It bathed the cluttered, tomb-sized room in a ghastly artificial glow. Grotesque shadows slithered across the cold, bleak walls. Sleep was impossible for Ben. He was afraid that if he closed his eyes, he'd never wake up again. Every nerve in his emaciated carcass buzzed with an edgy hunger that ached deep in his brittle bones.

Ben tossed and moaned as he clutched his distended abdomen and muttered, "The juice. The bloody juice."

He wanted to jump out of his dry, raw skin. Instead, he shot up like a steel spring had snapped in his back. Then he leaped to the floor and crouched on his haunches like an animal. His eyes burned wild and red in their dark, hollow sockets. They darted back and forth and fixed on a roll of thick nylon cord. He lurched across the room and seized the cord with his bony fingers. The rational scientist had become a demented creature. He clinched the cord in his teeth and crawled on his hands and knees to the cot where Curtis slept peacefully. He lashed the cord securely to one of the legs of the sturdy aluminum cot, then slid the cord underneath and wrapped it around Curtis' heaving chest. It was snug, but not tight enough to disturb his sleeping roommate. He repeated the maneuver slowly and silently until he had worked his way down to Curtis' ankles. He tied the loose end of the cord to a metal leg at foot of the cot and stepped back to admire his work.

Inhuman glee consumed Eaton. He tried to contain himself, but couldn't. A maniacal chuckle rumbled deep inside his emaciated chest. He clinched his jaws tight and tried to hold it in. That only made it more hideous as it wheezed through the gaps in his sinister grin. He hopped around the the room and beat the cold concrete floor with his fist. The dull thuds were masked by an endless stream of dog show commentary that droned from the TV in the corner. Eaton frantically glanced around the room. He found what he was looking for. Above the door, on the top shelf of some narrow industrial shelving, the object of his unwholesome attention waited patiently for use. It was the medical kit. He leapt to his feet and wrestled the large molded plastic box to the floor. Eaton fumbled with the clasp and popped the lid. There were enough supplies inside to perform a major operation—and Eaton knew how to use them all. He trained as a medic for this assignment and his advanced life science degree required him to take countless pre-med courses.

Eaton rifled through the box until he found what he was looking for: a bottle of novocaine, a hypodermic needle, a butterfly bandage, and a small scalpel. He gathered his supplies and scooted to the foot of Curtis' cot, then gently lifted the bottom of the thick gray blanket and exposed Curtis' large bare feet. He carefully removed a thick wool sock from his partner's hot damp foot. It was plump, pink, and naked. Eaton was ecstatic. He spun around in circles and growled. His hands shook with anticipation as he ripped off the paper cover to the disposable hypodermic with his teeth. Then he popped the plastic cap that shielded the slender needle with a flick of his thumb. It flew across the room and rolled under a table. Then he plunged the hollow needle into the soft, pink, rubber center on the novocaine bottle's cap. He drew off a small quantity of the clear liquid as he held the bottle upside-down. When he'd drawn enough, he pulled the needle out and squirted some of the local anesthetic in the air.

Eaton aimed the sharp needle at the pudgy big toe on Curtis' left foot and slowly moved in closer. When the hollow needle point pierced the tough, yet yielding flesh, it made a faint squishy pop. Eaton expertly injected the novocaine into the bottom of the tender toe. Curtis stirred, but didn't awake. Eaton waited a few moments for the anesthetic to take effect, then removed the small scalpel from its sterile plastic sleeve. It was sharper than any razor blade. A kaleidoscope of flashing colors from the TV screen shimmered on its keen cutting edge. He clutched the bulbous toe and plunged the scalpel into its meaty underside. He sliced deeper and thrust downward with one sure stroke. The moist callused skin was no match for the surgical steel. It split open like a round, ripe fig.

The incision was deep and clean. Blood gushed from the gaping wound. Eaton dropped the scalpel and positioned his head under the warm red spring of blood that flowed from the obscene gash. He closed his eyes and opened his mouth wide. The sweet, salty serum splashed into his mouth and splattered over his cheeks and chin. But too much of the precious life sustaining fluid was being wasted. Eaton dropped to his knees and approached the gory gusher from above. He popped the entire toe in his mouth and pursed his thin, cracked lips tight

around the plump, hairy shaft. He began to suck the blood with a strong even suction. It flowed freely over his tongue and spilled down his parched gullet. It was rich and thick. The vegetarian turned vampire moaned with delight.

Curtis' eyes sprang open. Something was wrong—very wrong. At first the unsuspecting blood donor was disoriented—half asleep. When Curtis tried to move, he realized he was trussed up like a pig on its way to slaughter.

He called out in confusion, "Ben! What the fuck's going on?"

There was no answer, just a sickening slurping sound. His foot felt strange and numb. He pressed his chin to his chest and raised his head enough to see Eaton nursing his big toe like a hideous bony baby. Curtis struggled and cursed. Eaton's eyes fluttered open, then drooped in loathsome contentment. They peered through Curtis rather than at him in an ominous Antarctic stare. Eaton kept sucking. The regular rhythm of the slurping lulled him into a sleepy state of ecstasy. His eyes rolled back in their sockets as he moaned with sickening satisfaction.

Curtis screamed, "STOP! Untie me, you sick fuck!"

Eaton snapped out of his cozy trance and stopped sucking. His head shot upright with a quick reptilian jerk. A menacing grin spread across his gaunt face. He bared his blood streaked teeth and pale diseased gums, then giggled fiendishly. Coagulated blood bubbled between his broad crooked incisors and spilled over his narrow cracked lips.

He wiped his chin with the back of his hand, "That's enough for now. I feel muuuch better."

Curtis arched his back and tried to break the bonds. It was no use. The thick nylon cord wouldn't yield. He was wrapped like a mummy. Eaton grabbed the bloody toe and squeezed the gushing incision closed. Then he licked it clean and cinched it tight with a butterfly bandage. The stream of blood slowed to a trickle, then stopped. He wiggled the toe playfully and tickled the bottom of Curtis' foot.

With a crude attempt at an Eastern European dialect, Ben gibed, "Like Bela Lugosi used to say, *the blood is the life, Mr. Renfield.*"

It was obvious that Eaton had lost his mind.

Curtis was at the mercy of a madman, so he tried to humor him, "That whole blood idea was brilliant. I don't know why we didn't think of it sooner. We'll have to do it again some time. Untie me and we can watch some TV."

Eaton rocked back and forth, growling and giggling. Frothy scarlet bubbles gurgled from his lips with each bloody burp.

He shook his head, "Oh no. You're staying right where you are."

"Come on, release me, Eaton. I can't see the TV like this."

Eaton quickly snapped back, "I'll fix that," as he dragged a chair over to the head of his prisoner's cot.

With surprising strength, he raised it at an angle and shoved a chair in place to keep it at an incline. Curtis' violated toe throbbed as the blood rushed to his lower extremities.

Curtis pleaded, but Eaton wasn't listening. He just watched TV and giggled.

After the soap operas were over, the toe-sucking psychopath sprang to his feet and sang, "*Lunch time.*"

Eaton crouched at the foot of his helpless friend's cot, then popped up like a hellish, jaundiced, Jack-in-the-box. He gleefully peeled back the bloody bandage on his unwilling wet-nurse's swollen, purple toe. Eaton grunted and pinched the aching wound. It popped open like a soft plastic coin purse. The savage vegetarian's hungry eyes widened as blood gushed from the clean, deep slit. Eaton quivered in anticipation, then began nursing. The brutish suction and nauseating slurping was more than Curtis could take. He shuddered in disgust and clinched his fists. When the ordeal was over, Eaton returned to their usual viewing routine—until it was time for dinner. More nursing, then more TV—then more nursing again. The sickening

feeding cycle went on for days. Curtis eventually became numb to the horror and accepted it with grim resignation.

Eaton looked a little better, but not much. There was a hint of color in his sunken cheeks, but his mental faculties had deteriorated considerably. Once or twice a day, he'd turn on the radio, put on the headphones and babble incoherently into the microphone. Sometimes he'd dance around the room and mouth the words to heavy metal rock videos. When his girlfriend came on the news, he'd pull down his pants and hump the set. It was impossible for Curtis to talk to him anymore. Any communication between them was totally one-sided. Eaton had become a monstrous, inhuman fiend.

The hemoglobin-hungry parasite hadn't nursed for two days, when he suddenly pounced on his unwilling host's chest. He leered down at Curtis and ranted in an incoherent tirade. Curtis turned his head to avoid the foul smelling shower of rancid drool that dripped with every delirious word.

Eaton gestured wildly, "I know what you're thinking. You think I'm crazy. You think I'm going to die soon. Then you'll eat me. I'll show you. You'll be sorry. Your blood is poison. It's killing me."

Eaton leaped from his victim's chest and circled the perimeter of the cramped room like a caged beast. Then he pounced on the medical kit and riffled through its frightening contents. He muttered to himself as he organized an ominous assortment of surgical devices on the grimy floor. Neat little piles of sterile packages fanned out in a semicircle at the madman's feet. The unwholesome purpose of the unfamiliar bottles and boxes was a mystery to Curtis. But he was certain of one thing—he wasn't going to like it much. In the center of the sinister arrangement was a foreboding orthopedic saw. Its sharp, serrated teeth had an appetite for living flesh—and so did Eaton. Curtis began to sweat.

The blood thirsty maniac mumbled to himself, "I'll show

you, Mr. Meat. You and your animal protein and your junk food. You like meat? I'll show you meat!"

Curtis screamed and thrashed from side to side on his urine soaked cot. He was helpless, totally vulnerable to his rabid partner's ghastly whims and appetites. Eaton ripped open one of the packages and removed a large hypodermic. He rummaged through his supplies, found a bottle of morphine and filled the syringe.

Curtis begged, "Please don't! Put that down. Let me go, please!"

Eaton yelled, "I want meat and I want it NOW!"

Curtis braced himself and waited for the bite of the cold, sharp needle and the horror that would surely follow. Since only his head and feet were exposed, he wondered where the needle would land. Eaton sat down near the head of the cot. It was now clear that he'd have to take it in the face, or maybe in the neck. His anus was so tight that his butt muscles cramped in a painful spasm. Curtis looked directly into his tormentor's crazy eyes. He was as ready as any sane man could be to die at the hands of a deranged cannibal.

But instead of jabbing the needle into Curtis, Eaton pulled up the sleeve of his tattered parka. Curtis watched in disbelief as Eaton plunged the hypodermic deep into a raised, blue vein in his own withered arm. The powerful opiate raced to Eaton's tortured brain as he slowly flexed his gangly biceps. Then a warm wave of ecstacy washed away the pain from every convolution in his squirming cortex. He threw his head back and sighed.

Curtis was stunned, "What the hell did you do that for?"

In a low woozy voice, Eaton answered, "Courage."

"You chicken shit son of a bitch. Do you mean to tell me that you need to get stoned before you have the guts to butcher me?"

The drug made Eaton somewhat lucid, "I'm not going to

butcher you, Curtis. I'd never eat your tainted meat. Your meat is poison—too many preservatives and toxins. I have my own meat. Pure meat. Sweet meat."

With that, Eaton ripped his right pant-leg up the middle and peeled it back. Tufts of white, fluffy insulation framed his cadaverous leg. It looked painfully naked in the unnatural light of the flickering television screen. He seized a rubber tourniquet and wrapped it around his emaciated leg—just bellow his bulbous knee. Then he thrust his leg out straight and cinched the tourniquet tight. Eaton grabbed the orthopedic saw and rested the razor sharp blade across the top of his bony shin. In the hands of a healer, the precision cutting tool would have been an instrument of mercy. In the hands of a maniac, it was the doorway to hell.

Eaton took a deep breath and began to saw at an awkward angle. As he ripped the blade back and forth, he howled and yelped like an injured dog. Perspiration poured from his forehead and ran down his chin. It mingled with the crimson puddle that grew larger with every agonizing stroke. Blood spattered on the walls and ceiling with each downward thrust. Grizzly globs of gore pelted Curtis as he lay helpless, weeping on his cot.

He watched in horror as Eaton persisted in his gruesome task. He screamed for him to stop, but his frantic pleas were drowned out when Eaton suddenly started humming the theme to the *Dick Van Dyke Show.* It was loud and out of tune, but it kept time to the cadence of the blade. Half way through, the bloody saw jammed in his dense shin. Eaton stoped and raised his leg enough to take the pressure off the deep, narrow gash. One long, slow backward stroke got him back on track. The wet grinding squeal of surgical steel on brittle bone reverberated in Curtis' spinal cord. He shivered with each rip of the cruel blade. Eaton had almost cut clean through when an uncooperative flap of skin at the back of his calf made him

stop. He grimaced and wrestled a delicate scalpel from its sterile paper sheath. A few quick slashes and the twitching leg was detached. It rolled over and plopped into the gruesome pond of bloody gristle—cold and slippery like a dead fish.

Eaton collapsed—pale and exhausted. He panted like a sick animal until he caught his breath. Acting more on some crude instinct than a conscious sense of purpose, he tucked his lifeless leg under his arm and scooted backwards to the corner of the room. He propped his hunger ravished carcass against the wall and and positioned his repellent prize in front of him. He hovered over it like a predator guarding its kill. Curtis watched his crippled friend in disbelief. A feeling of profound pity replaced the utter terror he felt only moments earlier. Ben glared at Curtis. The wild man snarled as he nibbled pulpy little strips of raw flesh from the mangled stump.

Curtis stared at the loathsome slab of meat and gristle and shook his head. The horrifying consequences of slow starvation that lay before him weren't nearly as hideous as one pathetic realization. His desperate friend's mutilated appendage was still wearing its thick wool sock and leather snow boot. If only Eaton had removed them, Curtis may have been able to forget. Now, he'd never be able to watch someone tap their foot to a tune or kick a football without thinking about Eaton's butchered leg. Was it even a leg any longer? It couldn't be used to take a walk in the park or bounce a baby. Now, it was just meat.

Curtis wondered where the meat left off and his friend began. At what point did the sum total of all the meaty parts add up to something more than sirloin? If he was sitting in a coffeehouse in Greenwich Village sipping espresso, the answer would come easily. In his frozen prison at the bottom of the world, he didn't have a clue.

Eaton dragged his severed leg to his lap. Then he reached in his pocket and pulled out the scalpel. He gouged out thick hairy chunks of pink, pulpy flesh and stuffed them into his greedy mouth. It was painful to watch him gnaw on the meaty hunks, but Curtis was afraid to look away from the grotesque feeding frenzy. There was no telling what his inhuman friend might do next. Eaton paused occasionally to dislodge clumps of coarse hair that stuck in his throat. He hawked them up like a cat with a hairball. After devouring more than half of his gruesome calf muscle, he pushed his ghastly meal away and grabbed the radio.

The pathetic glutton jabbered away for several minutes, then burped. It was a wet, rumbling burp that rose from deep inside his churning abdomen. His face turned white. Blood rushed to his stomach in a vain attempt to digest the loathsome feast. It was no use. Too many weeks had passed since he'd eaten anything—let alone rich, raw meat. One gurgling belch led to another. Eaton's back stiffened, his head jutted forward, his jaw dropped—then it all came up. He heaved every morbid mouthful of partially digested muscle. Carnage spewed from his gaping mouth as his frail body convulsed.

When the eruption subsided, Eaton was covered with bubbling globs of gore. He stared at the sinister suet in his lap and began to sob. With a violent sideways twist, he dumped his repulsive regurgitation on the floor. Something shiny glistened in the chunky pool of blood and puke—the scalpel. He fished it out and clinched it between his teeth. Then he slithered toward Curtis like a hideous maimed lizard. When he reached the cot, he pulled himself on top of Curtis. He jerked the scalpel under Curtis' chin. His helpless prey recoiled the inch or two his bonds permitted.

Eaton straddled his writhing prisoner, then leered and whispered, "I'm sorry."

Curtis shut his eyes and whimpered—grateful for an end to the torture. He heard the scalpel swish past his ear, then a dull slicing sound and a series of loud pops. The taught nylon cord yielded to the scalpel's keen cutting edge. It fell in curly white piles on either side of his cot. Curtis opened his eyes in time to see Ben awkwardly creep back to his bloody corner.

Curtis took a deep breath, stretched and sat-up slowly. He was stiff, but free. He glanced over at Ben. His pitiful friend clutched the tourniquet around his stump with one hand and juggled the remote with the other. He zapped through the channels until he found the news and stopped. There was his girlfriend, she was reporting a story about a woman who was seriously burned when she microwaved a raw egg and it blew up in her face. At the end of the story the corner of the enigmatic newswoman's mouth raised ever so slightly.

Ben smiled and said, "I love you, darling." He turned to Curtis and said, "Good-bye ol' buddy—I can't go on like this any more."

He tightened his grip on the rubber tourniquet.

Curtis yelled, "NO!"

Ben ripped the tourniquet off his mutilated stump. A fountain of blood gushed with incredible force. He lost consciousness instantly as his blood pressure dropped to zero. Curtis jumped to his feet and tried to run to Ben, but his legs crumpled under him. They were numb and weak from lack of circulation. He collapsed in the slippery pond of hemoglobin and horror that pooled over the entire floor. He dragged himself through the muck to Ben's blood soaked cot. There was nothing he could do. Ben was gone. Only the meat remained.

Ben's girlfriend fiddled with some papers, said good night and did that thing with her mouth. Curtis watched her closely. She *did* seem to know more than she was telling. Maybe she knew where Ben had gone. Curtis looked down at the twisted corpse on the cot. It was obvious where the meat was.

There was a lot do for the next few days. Curtis kept busy and tried not to think about Ben. He cleaned the grizzly living quarters, but didn't go near Ben's body. A heavy canvas tarp, tossed over his friend's twisted remains, substituted for a

proper burial. The body wouldn't decompose any time soon. There weren't enough bacteria in the room to rot a dead penguin. Even though it was heated, the room was still as cold as a walk-in freezer. The temperature outside had fallen drastically in the past few months. Now it stayed pitch black outside twenty-four hours a day. Curtis always wore his heavy insulated clothing and never ventured outside. He cranked up the TV volume to drown out the constant din of the homicidal polar wind. Every day he had to turn it up a little louder.

Curtis' viewing habits began to change. He had a major revelation as he watched an international ice skating competition. He was transfixed by the grace and agility of the beautiful female skaters. The allure of their powerful, yet feminine bodies held his undivided attention. But the longer he watched, the colder he became. After twenty minutes, he began to shiver. Then it hit him. He realized that there were basically three kinds of TV shows: cold shows, warm shows and neutral shows. Shows like *Bay Watch, Hawaii Five-0, Miami Vice, Magnum, P.I.,* and old beach movies were warm shows. *Northern Exposure, St. Elsewhere, Hill Street Blues,* winter sports and Bergman movies were all cold shows. Game shows, talk shows and the news were neutral. He decided to watch only warm shows with a smattering of the neutral shows now and then. Luckily his girlfriend had a warm show. The sweaty work-outs on the beach were just what he needed.

He joined in the exercises every morning and even improvised a crude set of weights. They were made from a sawed off mop handle and some heavy reference books—The Professor from *Gilligan's Island* would have been proud. He felt stronger and lighter with each passing day. His heavy survival clothing felt looser, but it was too cold to take them off to check his progress. He zapped through the channels, stopped at the all news network and turned on the hot-plate to boil a cup of water. Then he went into the closet-sized bathroom and screwed in the bare bulb that dangled over head. He looked in the mirror. Two startling eyes peered back at him through a thick mass of hair and grime. He looked like the Wolfman. The kettle whistled frantically. Instead of pouring the boiling water in his crusty cup, he emptied the whole pot into a deep ceramic bowl. He found some soap and a razor and went to work. The hot water felt good on his cold face and hands.

First he washed his long greasy black hair and tied it back in a ponytail. Then he scrubbed, lathered and shaved his face. The transformation was astounding.

He turned his head from side to side in disbelief and gawked at the face in the mirror, "Well who the hell are you?"

The guy in the mirror mouthed his words, but it wasn't him. It wasn't Curtis Hardy, the hulking, too tall blimp who never went out on dates. It wasn't the same Curtis Hardy who always smiled when some asshole made a crack about his weight. And it definitely wasn't Curtis "Lardy" Hardy who got the shit kicked out of him in grammar school and was always the last one picked for any team sport. The guy in the mirror had to be some big star who just happened to be doing a film on location in Antarctica and wandered in by mistake. Or maybe he was a lover boy from Beverly Hills named Chip or Chad, who drove a sports car and drilled buffed-out models. It couldn't be Curtis Hardy—but it was.

The only features he could recognize were his eyes. Actually, only the irises stayed the same. They were still blue. His puffy bags were gone and so were his fleshy lids. Something seemed different about his nose. It used to look too small, sandwiched between the massive mounds of fat on his cheeks. Now, the fat was gone and his nose was just the right size. Curtis was amazed to see that he had cheekbones—he never saw them before. They were high and angular. Then he noticed that he had only one chin instead of three. It was

strong and broad and looked like it could take a punch. Even his ears seemed different. They used to look stuck-on—like *Mr. Potato Head* ears. Now they were integrated into his facial architecture by his well defined jaw line and muscular neck. He ran his hands over the contours of his new face. Then he slapped it to make sure it was real. It stung and turned red. Curtis laughed and turned out the light.

He sat on his cot and watched the news-anchor recap the events of the day. The newsman glanced up from his notes, looked Curtis right in the eye and said, "Next up, a live report from the Earthwatch One rescue expedition in Christchurch, New Zealand."

Curtis jumped off his cot and ran to the TV. The reporter cut to a commercial. Curtis coaxed, "Come on, come on," as an aging rock star sang about his ice cold beer.

Then a woman's face filled the tiny screen. A pink, fur-lined, Patagonia parka hood framed her familiar features. It was Ben's girlfriend. A large microphone shook in her gloved hand.

Her voice quivered from the cold, "I'm coming to you live from Christchurch, New Zealand a thousand miles north of the frozen continent of Antarctica. For some, it's the last frontier, a land of frigid beauty and adventure. For others, it's an icy grave. Over the years, hundreds of explorers and scientists have sacrificed their lives in the search for knowledge. We are here today to witness the rescue of two brave environmental scientists, Dr. Benjamin Eaton and Dr. Curtis Hardy. They have not been heard from for six months. I have with me, Frank Sayer, Field Director of Environmental Defense International and leader of the Earthwatch One rescue expedition. Mr. Sayer, what are the chances that these men are still alive?"

The camera cut to Sayer, who looked like a cross between Admiral Byrd and an aging hippie Eskimo. He was stiff and self-conscious.

His eyes darted from side to side as he lisped into the microphone, “There ith a good chanth they’re thtill alive. They’re rethourceful, well equipped and profethional. They have adequate food and thelter. If the weather holdth, we thould reach Earthwatch One in 48 houth.”

The newswoman stopped him before he could utter another garbled word, “Well, we won’t keep you any longer, Mr. Sayer. I know you have a lot to do before you leave for Antarctica.” The wind blew back the hood of her parka, “We’ll have more as this story unfolds. Now back to our studios in Atlanta.”

Curtis was ecstatic. He started talking to the canvas covered heap of gore in the corner, “Did you hear that, Ben? We’re getting out of here. We’re going home!”

The next two days passed slowly—hours seemed like weeks. He tried to busy himself by writing a report on the nuclear cover-up and watching the news. Finally the moment he’d been waiting for arrived.

The newsman said, “We interrupt our normal broadcast for this special report.”

Shaky video footage of the the devastated compound filled the screen. The picture was fuzzy and Ben’s girlfriend sounded like she was talking from a phone booth on the dark side of the Moon. The harsh camera lights tunneled through the darkness. Earthwatch One looked worse then he remembered. The twisted metal structures and charred debris made it look like a ship wreck at the bottom of a frozen sea.

The rescue team descended the icy steps as the door to the sleeping quarters came into view. They pounded hard. Curtis jumped like a startled cat. For a moment he’d forgotten that he was watching his own rescue—live via satellite. He ran to the door and pushed as the rescuers pulled from the outside. The door flew open. A fierce polar wind forced him backwards. The temperature dropped a hundred degrees instantly. The

sound was deafening. In a heartbeat the room filled with people. Curtis was blinded by the glaring camera lights. He shielded his eyes and instinctively looked down at the TV. There he was, shielding his eyes, looking at the TV that showed him shielding his eyes as he looked at an infinity of TVs. His eyelids began to flutter. Bright silver stars sparkled in his dimming cone of vision. Then everything went black.

When Curtis regained consciousness, he was stretched out on his cot. Half a dozen people peered down at him. They were all talking at once and arguing about what to do. Curtis recognized some of them: Frank Sayer, Neva Dunette, and of course Ben's girlfriend.

Finally Sayer yelled, "Okay, everybody clear out! Give the poor thon of a bitch thome room. Neva, you thtay here and get him cleaned up. Everybody elth—OUT! We'll wait in the thnow vehicleth."

Sayer herded them through the thick metal door one by one, then slammed it closed behind him.

There was a long awkward silence. Neva didn't know what to say. Neither did Curtis, he hadn't logged much alone-time with members of the opposite sex. Neva noticed the hot plate and put a pot of water on to boil.

Curtis broke the ice with small talk, "So, how are things back at EDI?"

"Fine," She stared at the pot and waited for the water to boil.

"What's the matter with Sayer? He talks funny."

"It's a long story. He hurt his tongue last week. It needed seven stitches."

Curtis fiddled with the draw-string on his parka,"I remember you from last summer—the oil spill in Maine."

"Yea, you brought a case of chocolate cupcakes and wouldn't let anyone near them."

"That was me, Curtis 'Lardy' Hardy." He slapped his stomach, but it wasn't there.

Neva looked around the room, "Do you have any soap and a washcloth or something?"

"There's some soap in the bathroom. I don't think we have any washcloths."

Neva picked up a large natural sponge from a galvanized bucket, "This'll do." She came back with the soap. When the water began to bobble, she poured it into the bucket. "This is too hot. I'll cool it off."

Curtis lifted his head and cautioned, "Don't cool it off too much. Water doesn't stay hot very long down here."

She laughed and took off her lavender parka. Underneath, she was wearing an old grey sweatshirt with the Columbia University insignia on the front. The old fashioned emblem took on an unexpected graphic appeal as it rose and fell over the contours of her high, firm breasts. She pushed up her sleeves and unzipped her heavy insulated pants. Curtis felt his heart race as she wiggled out of them. She had a well-worn pair of Levi's on underneath. The loose fitting denim could not conceal the gentle curves of her well rounded hips. A beaded Indian belt snaked through the loops and squeezed her tiny waist tight. Neva tossed back her soft reddish-brown hair and dropped the soap and sponge into the bucket. The steaming water sloshed from side to side as she slowly walked toward Curtis. She looked like she was going to wash her car on a sunny summer afternoon. Curtis tensed as she set the bucket down and knelt beside him.

Neva was nervous. She fumbled with the zipper of Curtis' gamy brown parka. It was jammed tight under his chin. A sideways tug got it back on track. As she slowly pulled it down, steam rose from the widening V-shaped gap. Her face flushed as the bulky coat fell open. She hadn't expected to find such a well sculptured body inside. Curtis' chest was a broad expanse of well defined muscle. His stomach was taught and flat. His skin glistened with perspiration. She continued to peel back the dingy parka and removed his heavy padded pants. A metamorphosis had taken place. Curtis emerged from his crusty cocoon. When he had put on the heavy nylon chrysalis six months earlier, he was a bloated, human larva. Now he was magnificent. His body was perfect. As he rose from the cot, Neva stood up and stepped back. Her eyes wandered across the rugged landscape of his fantastic physique. She explored every rolling hill and hidden valley. There was so much to see. Neva had never seen a man, her own age, naked before. Her body reacted before she had a chance to think or speak. A sudden fire burned below her navel and radiated down her thighs. Muscles she never knew she had contracted deep inside her. Curtis folded his powerful arms across his huge chest.

He shivered and said, "If you're going to sponge me off—do it. I'm freezing."

Neva jerked and looked away, "Yea, right. Of course. I'm sorry." She reached down in the bucket and grabbed the sponge, then squeezed out some of the steamy water and lathered it with soap. Curtis turned around. She ran the sponge across the broad expanse of his strong shoulders. The hot, soapy water cascaded in steaming sheets down his rippling back. It tumbled down the tight crevice of his muscular butt like a waterfall, then trickled over his sturdy legs and splashed on the cold grey floor. Curtis raised his arms above his head. Neva scrubbed sensuously and wished that she was the sponge. He turned around and faced Neva. She plunged the sponge into the hot water, held it over his head and squeezed it out. It poured down all six feet four inches of his hard body. She scrubbed the front of him with increasing fervor. His male equipment had retreated from the cold. It was riding high and compact. But as the warm water spilled over his cool tool, it dropped and began to swell.

Neva had never witnessed that particular anatomical phenomenon before. She wanted to see more so she brushed it

with the side of her soapy arm and scrubbed all around the area of her interest. Each time she did, it dropped lower and swelled more. Curtis inched his legs apart to make room for his growing manhood. He looked down at Neva. As she leaned forward, the loose neck of her baggy sweatshirt swooped down and revealed her soft white breasts. He never realized a woman's nipples could get so long. His heart pounded and his cock throbbed as it rose and stiffened. Neva dropped the sponge and ran her slender fingers over its swollen tip and down its long, thick shaft. It bobbed up and down as her fingers neared the hilt. She wanted to grab it and she did. Neva was startled by its length and girth as it throbbed in her hand. It was hard, but smooth as velvet to the touch. She reached down and cupped his warm orbs in the palm of her other hand. They were heavy and tight. She squeezed gently—Curtis moaned. An urgent emptiness ached inside her.

Neva quickly unfastened her belt buckle and pulled her pants down without bothering to unzip them. They tumbled around her ankles. Her practical, white cotton panties weren't absorbent enough to contain the hot lusty juice that ran down her smooth inner thighs. Delicate white wisps of condensation rose from the moist heat that radiated from the aching center of her desire.

Neva threw her arms around Curtis' strong neck and straddled one of his hard bulging thighs. She pressed her pubic bone deep into his muscular leg. He felt the eager pressure of her hot, wet feminine anatomy. It slid up and down easily on his well lubricated quadriceps. Curtis wrapped his arms around her and squeezed. Neva moaned and rode his massive thigh as if it were a wild stallion. The door suddenly burst open. Sayer and the newswoman rushed in and slammed it closed behind them. Neva was in another world. She just kept moaning and humping. Curtis smiled at his unexpected guests and shrugged with his eyes.

They stood there speechless, then Sayer yelled, “Neva Dunette, thtop that right now! For Chritht thake, I told you to clean him up, not rub him raw with your cunt. He’s a thick man!”

Neva screamed and whipped around. When she saw her boss and the newswoman, she bolted for the bathroom. She only waddled a few steps, with her pants around her ankles, before she fell down. Curtis helped her to her feet.

As she wiggled into her pants, Curtis said, “It’s really my fault, Sayer. I got carried away.”

Neva was mortified. She covered her face and began to sob.

Sayer softened, “Thtop crying. Everybody doeth it. We all get hot panth thome timeth. Let’th get the hell out of here before the weather changeth.”

Sayer handed Curtis some fresh survival clothes. The newswoman sat on the tarp covered mound of gore on the cot in the corner. She planted her tight, shapely butt down hard, there was a squishy crunching sound. She wiggled several times to get comfortable and started scribbling notes on a long yellow pad. Curtis tied his hood and zipped his parka. Neva had regained her composure and looked at the map with Sayer.

Curtis finished lacing his boots and said, “Okay, I’m ready. Let’s get out of here.”

Sayer gestured at the TV, “Aren’t you going to turn that damn thing off?”

Curtis felt a chill go up his spine, “I’d rather not, if you don’t mind.”

Everyone turned their attention to the tiny television. Alex Trebeck informed three tense contestants that it was time for *Final Jeopardy* and they could wager all or part of their winnings.

The business-like host said, “Our final category is—Greek mythology.” He glanced at the card in his hand, “The answer is: the Greek god who charmed the beasts with his song.”

Neva looked at Curtis. He shook his head and smiled.

Sayer blurted out, "ORPHEUTH!"

Curtis corrected him, "*Who* is Orpheus?"

Sayer was annoyed, "He'th the guy with the fucking harp!"

Curtis laughed, "I just meant that you must answer in the form of a question."

Sayer looked confused.

The news woman added, "He's right, Frank; Alex is a real stickler about that."

Curtis nodded, "Yea, and Art Flemming was even tougher. I've seen him practically rip a contestant's head off for not answering in the form of a correct question."

Sayer looked at them like they were both insane and exploded, "Who the fuck careth! Here'th *your* final jeopardy question: They all frothe to death in Antarctica because they were too fucking thtupid to leave."

Neva raised her hand, "*Who* is us?"

Sayer crooned, "Thath right—us. Oh, that remindth me, Hardy. Where ith Eaton? I athume he'th dead, but he mutht have died rethently. Collin Farr got a radio methage from him a couple of weekth ago. Did you bury hith body in the thnow?

Curtis shook his head, "No."

"Well then, where the hell ith he?"

The newswoman stopped writing and looked at Curtis.

Curtis pointed to where she was sitting, "He's over there, on the cot—under the tarp."

The newswoman jumped to her feet, grabbed her butt and screamed, "HOLY SHIT!"

She stuck her ass out and whipped her head around to see if any cadaver goo got on her well-rounded cheeks.

Curtis tried to reassure her, "Don't worry, ma'am. Believe me, Ben wouldn't mind." He searched for the right words and added, "He admired your work as a journalist—immensely. You were his favorite newsperson."

She didn't hear a word he said. The frantic newswoman

just kept swatting her butt with her yellow pad—even though nothing was there.

Curtis walked over and pulled the tarp off the putrid pile in the corner. The rescue party gagged and choked. Ben stared up at them with dry, sightless eyes. His jaw gaped open. Clotted blood and gore caked his ghastly mouth. His partially devoured leg rested sideways across his sunken chest. The newswoman stared at the monstrous corpse, then looked at Curtis. She did that funny little thing with her mouth and hurried off to find her cameraman. Neva's eyes darted back and forth between Ben's half eaten leg and his twisted mouth. Then she groaned and smacked her forehead in sudden recognition.

Neva turned to Sayer and gasped, "That radio message that Eaton sent—he wasn't saying 'I hate myself.' He was saying *I ATE MYSELF!*"

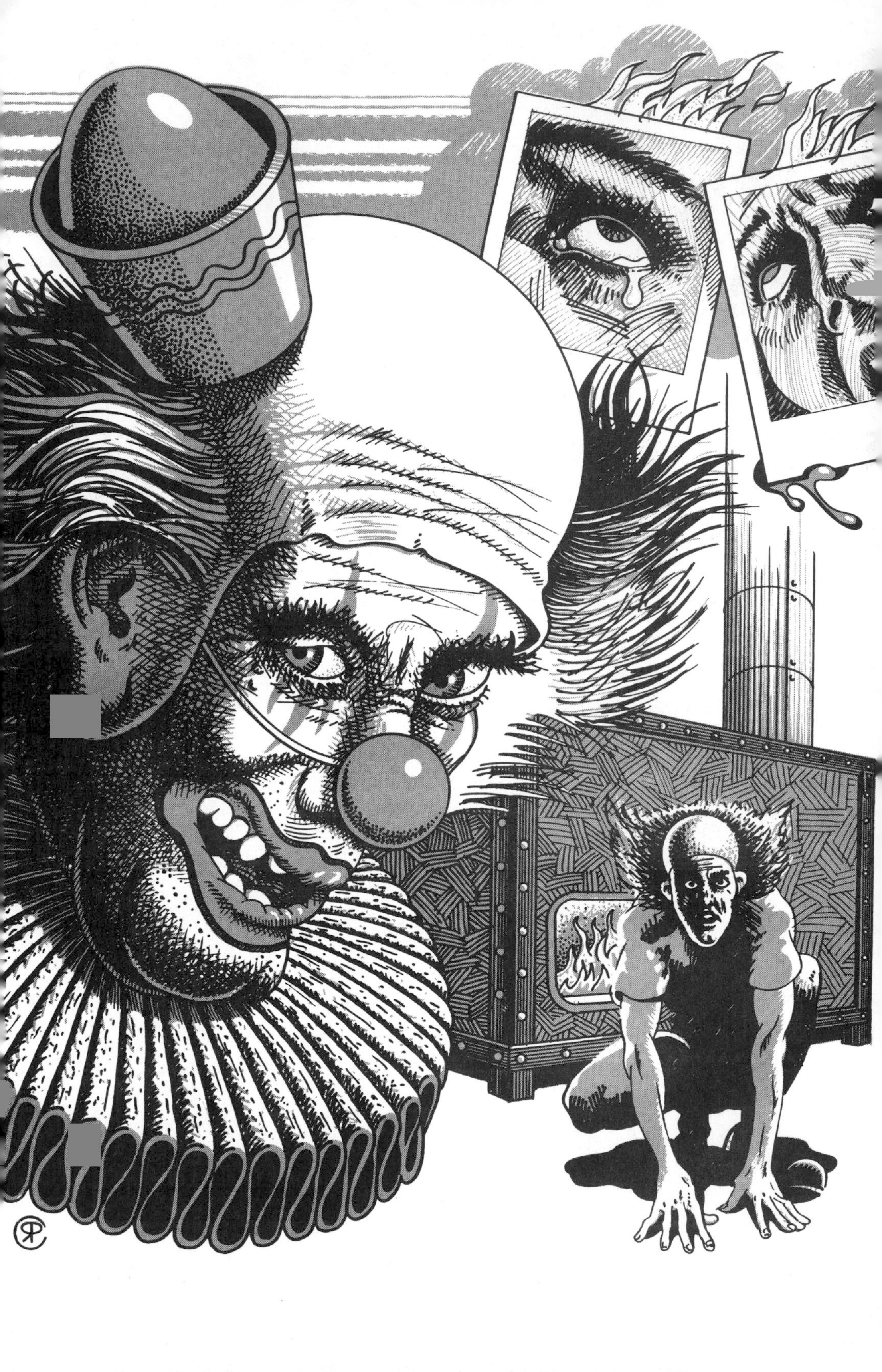

CLOWNS

I envy those who live a life
  Where nothing strange takes place;
The lucky ones whose days and nights
  Slip by without a trace.

At one time I was one of them.
  I never really knew
That horror waits at every turn
  And nightmares can come true.

By random chance or dark design,
My ordered life was thrown
Into a state of dread and fear
That I had never known.

It happened three short years ago,
October thirty-first.
Of all the nights that I've lived through,
That night alone was cursed.

I'd finished up a business trip
And I was heading home.
I'd finalized a contract with
the Houston Astrodome.

My company makes souvenirs—
T-shirts, pins and hats.
The Astros bought our brand new line—
Collector baseball bats.

I told my wife that I'd be back
In Denver late that night.
I drove through Northern Texas fast.
The autumn moon was bright.

The interstate was long and flat.
The night was warm and dry.
The restful rhythm of the road
Was like a lullaby.

I nodded off, then jerked awake.
  I'd driven much too long.
So I pulled off the interstate—
  Where I did not belong.

I made a turn, then turned again
  Down dusty, dark dirt roads—
Saw armadillos, bats and snakes,
  Heard crickets, owls and toads.

Beside the road, an old hotel,
  Ten miles from any town,
Lay rotting in the grim landscape—
  That's where I saw the clown.

I thought that I was seeing things.
  He ran in front of me.
I swerved in time to miss the fool
  And almost hit a tree.

My headlights stopped him in his tracks,
  Just like a startled deer.
He stood there with his big shoes on
  And evil grease paint sneer.

His eyes were round and red and wild.
  He pointed to the sky.
The clown began to hop around—
  Pretending he could fly.

He flapped his big arms up and down,
Then tapped my window hard.
He honked his red nose several times
And handed me his card.

His name was Bouncing Benny Brown
From Twin Falls, Idaho.
He pointed to the old hotel
And said, "Come on, let's go."

Reluctantly, I let him in
And drove across a field.
We neared the crumbling edifice—
He clapped and laughed and squealed.

We pulled up to the hotel door.
He thanked me for the ride;
Then handed me a bright green wig
And said, "Come on inside."

The reason why I followed him
Is still unclear to me.
I felt a strange euphoria—
A dark and haunting glee.

A clown on stilts stood by the door,
His face was broad and fat.
He greeted us, then waved us in
And tipped his doorman's hat.

My senses were assaulted by
A deafening, giddy din,
The sickening smell of pungent sweat,
And garish painted skin.

As we moved through the lobby slow,
A skull-faced little clown
Was leering at my normal clothes.
He looked me up and down.

I quickly put my green wig on
And fluffed the nylon hair.
I forced a phony, nervous smile
And wished I wasn't there.

The hotel had an atmosphere
Of danger, dread and doom;
And even though I needed rest,
I didn't want a room.

We pushed our way through crowds of clowns
Of every shape and size;
And though they all were quite unique,
They all had crazy eyes.

Above the yawning ballroom door
I saw a sign that read:
Psycho-Killer Cannibal Clowns
Convention~Straight Ahead

I laughed and turned to Benny Brown,
The sign seemed like a joke.
He looked confused and grinned at me,
Then licked his lips and spoke.

"Just think of us as hunters, friend,"
His voice gave me a chill.
"We never waste a single life—
We always eat our kill.

We stalk our prey at carnivals,
The circus and the fair.
At children's parties, look around,
You'll often find us there.

If they believe you're one of us,
You might leave here alive.
You'd better play along, my friend
Or you will not survive."

He dragged me to the ballroom floor
Where psycho killer clowns
Assembled by the hundreds from
Their sleepy little towns.

They beamed with ghoulish grease paint grins
As terror tales were told.
Their gory stories were insane,
Malicious, cruel and cold.

A blue-haired, brutish, drunk buffoon
Was boasting to the crowd
That once he ate some high school kids.
The clowns all laughed out loud.

He passed around some Polaroids.
The prints were smeared with blood.
One half-devoured victims' corpse
Was face-down in the mud.

I feigned that I was interested
As I thumbed through the stack
Of picture trophies showing him
Slash and stab and hack.

One grizzly photo clearly showed
A young girl with a crown.
The pretty prom queen's severed head
Was chopped off by the clown.

Then Benny slapped him on the back
And gave a knowing nod.
He cleared his throat and spoke up loud—
His voice was low and odd,

"Dear clowns and colleagues, can I have
Your full attention, please?
These pictures are magnificent,
But take a look at these."

He winked and started taking off
His circus-colored vest,
Then opened up his baggy blouse,
And bared his hairy chest.

A strange thing hung 'round Benny's neck.
It dangled in a loop.
The other clowns all oohed and aahed
As Benny charmed the group.

A closer look at what he wore
Confirmed my deepest fears.
What looked like dried up apricots
Were really shriveled ears.

He'd made a necklace out of them
With bones and beads and teeth.
He twirled around so all could see
The decomposing wreath.

He bowed and fingered them with pride,
Then turned to me and said,
"I cut my victim's right ear off
Before I make them dead.

It comforts me to keep them close.
Each one's a patient friend.
I talk to them when I'm alone—
They listen without end."

The savage clowns were all impressed.
  I thought that I might scream.
Their rowdy cheers and jealous sneers
  Made Bouncing Benny beam.

A paunchy Punchinello yelled,
"Attention, one and all,
Our dinner's finally being served
  Inside the banquet hall."

Then Bouncing Benny grabbed my arm
  And pulled me off my feet,
"Come on get movin'," Benny said,
  "I'm hungry—Let's go eat!"

I'm sure the hall was elegant—
  A century ago.
But now it reeked of foul debris
  That rotted down below.

Their decorations were grotesque.
  Intestines draped the hall.
A rude collage of body parts
  Was hung on every wall.

A string of severed human hands
  Swung from a chandelier.
They cast a ghastly shadow show
  Of light and dark and fear.

The tablecloths were tattooed skin,
  Arranged in odd designs.
The knives and forks were carved from bones.
  The candle sticks were spines.

An army of tuxedoed clowns
  Brought hors d'oeuvres on a tray.
The severed tongues in a blood clot sauce
  Made quite a foul display.

A heavy hunchbacked harlequin,
  With teeth filed razor sharp,
Played eerie dinner music on
  A human rib cage harp.

The clowns were waiting in a line
  For bloody smorgasbord.
They butchered all the hotel staff
  To feed their hungry hoard.

The steaming bins of half-cooked meat
  Were disappearing quick.
The way they gnawed the thick, red flesh
  Was making me feel sick.

They gorged themselves and passed foul gas,
  Spit gristle, bone and hair.
They belched and drooled, then ate some more—
  The gore was everywhere.

A bowl of steaming hearts arrived.
  The ghastly clowns dug in.
But when they munched on baby toes
  My head began to spin.

I fainted like a debutante
  And slid down to the floor.
When I woke up, I looked around
  And saw an open door.

I hid beneath the tabletop
  While Bouncing Benny ate
And gossiped with his fiendish friends.
  I knew I couldn't wait.

I inched toward the door outside
  Through table-legs and feet.
They didn't see me slip away.
  Their eyes were on their meat.

But as I crawled, I kicked a skull—
  A candle burned inside.
The fire danced across the floor—
  The planks were old and dried.

The fire crept up tablecloths
  And leaped from chair to chair.
The bloated clowns burst into flames
  And wailed in wild despair.

I bounded through the open door
  As flames engulfed the hall.
The sizzling clowns were trapped inside.
  The fire cooked them all.

I stumbled through the open field.
  The hotel belched out smoke.
The stench from those cremated clowns
  Caused me to gag and choke.

Some waddled from the old hotel;
  Their costumes in a blaze.
They broiled and screamed out in the dark.
  I stood there in a daze.

Then from the fierce inferno ran
  A clown consumed in flame.
He made his way to where I stood
  As he called out my name.

He lunged at me as I backed up,
  Then tumbled to the ground
And curled up in a smoking heap.
  He shrieked and writhed around.

I knew that it was Benny Brown—
  I can't imagine how.
There wasn't much of Benny left.
  I still can see him now.

The fire seared and charred his flesh.
His burned and blackened bones
Protruded through his blistered meat.
His eyes were sightless stones.

With all the strength that he had left,
He raised a glowing hand
And coughed as he began to speak.
I tried to understand.

He sighed, "The hunger . . ." then he paused.
Black smoke was in his breath.
"The hunger made me do bad things."
The clown was close to death.

"Don't give in to the hunger, friend."
His lips cracked off like coal.
"The hunger gets inside of you,
And eats away your soul."

He said, "Thanks for the fire, friend,"
And simmered like a roast.
His embers swirled around my feet
As he gave up the ghost.

I waited there a long, long time,
Until the clowns were dead.
Each twisted brain lay smoldering
Inside a haunted head.

The darkness of the desert night
Snuffed out the dying flames.
The fire had destroyed the clowns
And only left their names:

Joe Jigs the Clown and Benny Brown
And Topsy from Saint Paul,
Rags Malone and Jolly Joan
Were all I could recall.

I made my way through smoking piles
Of soot and bones and shoes.
I couldn't help but think about
Those stories on the news.

The ones where people disappear
And never can be found.
How many were the victims of
Those ashes on the ground?

I suddenly felt numb and ill.
The air was dry and cold.
The morning sun lit up the sky
With blue and pink and gold.

My face and hands were covered with
A smoky, oily grime—
The evil, reeking residue
Of homicidal slime.

It soaked into my skin and bones
And everything between.
I knew that if I washed for days—
I never would get clean.

I found my car and drove away;
  But I was not secure.
I knew I'd left with memories
  That I could not endure.

Since then, there hasn't been a day
  I've felt completely right.
I always think about those clowns
  And what I saw that night.

Sometimes I wake up in the night
  From dreams about that place—
The dismal Texas wasteland
  And Benny's burning face.

His charred lips whisper obscene things
  That make me feel afraid.
And even after I wake up
  My fears refuse to fade.

At midnight every Halloween
  And when the moon is big,
I go down in my basement and
  Put on my bright green wig.

I lock the doors and windows tight
  While trick-or-treaters play—
And crouch behind the furnace till
  The hunger goes away.

Hawaiian Hamburgers

It was almost feeding time at Baxter's Burger Hut, home of The Hawaiian Burger. An edgy stillness permeated the over-decorated atmosphere of the tiny burger joint. It was like the silent beat before a predator pounces on its prey. Mr. Baxter glanced at his watch as he held the artificial bamboo door open for his only employee. Bruce Fowler stumbled awkwardly through the doorway as he fumbled with the buttons on his regulation Hawaiian shirt. It was exactly 3:45 p.m., right on time, as usual. Bruce was a strange boy, but he was punctual. Every day after school, he rushed to the Burger Hut—a step ahead of his carnivorous classmates. They swept down from the high school on the hill like a pack of ravenous wolves. They were rabid for Hawaiian hamburgers. Luckily the burgers weren't as tasteless as the tropical decor.

The mismatched hodgepodge of South Sea motifs was enough to make Don Ho puke. It was a tropical nightmare of burnt cork, fishing nets and generic Tikis. But the rickety cabaña-style shack was a money machine for Billy Ray Baxter. The old cowboy hit pay-dirt in Eldon, Iowa when he opened the Burger Hut. He'd never been west of Arizona, but he yearned to feel the trade winds blow his thinning gray-blond hair. He had created an isolated outpost of quasi-Polynesian culture in the sprawling Mid-West. And that was as close as he

was going to get to black sand beaches and topless native dancing girls. In some strange way, Baxter's primal culinary odyssey to the South Pacific made sense to the residents of Eldon—even when snow covered the Burger Hut's thatched roof.

Today, it almost seemed natural. It was mid-June, hot, humid, and the last day of school. The crowd was larger than usual and the feeding frenzy was more frantic. The graduating seniors of Westmont High assembled at the Burger Hut to make last minute arrangements for their senior prom, later that evening. Bruce was graduating too, but he had no arrangements to make. He was going to the prom, but not to have fun. He'd be working. Mr. Baxter was catering the event and Bruce would be there to help. He tried to get a date for the prom, but Bruce fell far short of any girl's dream of a perfect prom partner.

Bruce was a sullen teen. He never smiled and always kept to himself. Nature had not been particularly cruel to him. He wasn't a bad looking boy, just awkward and too tall for his age. His real problem was his unbelievably negative attitude and the bizarre behavior it produced. Bruce wasn't unpopular. Everyone at school knew him and was as friendly as his sour disposition allowed.

His classmates attributed his gloomy demeanor to his parents' professions. His father was the local exterminator and his mother worked as a part-time cosmetician at the only mortuary in town. Seventeen years of shop talk at the dinner table had taken its toll— Bruce was damaged goods.

Over the years he developed a repertoire of remarkably nasty habits and bizarre mannerisms. Eventually they merged to produce a repulsive little ritual. A nervous skin condition covered Bruce with hundreds of tiny scabs. The open sores were either bleeding, infected, or both. They never healed because he spent every waking moment picking them. He kept the nails on his thumb and forefinger exceptionally long for that express purpose. The spooky nails were thick, jagged and caked with clotted blood. When the coagulated muck became noticeable, Bruce would scrape it clean with his bottom incisors. He'd grind the revolting residue in a series of quick little rat bites, then hawk up some phlegm and gurgle it around with the scab-mush. When this operation was complete, he'd extend his neck like a turtle and swallow the morbid mixture with an audible gulp. With his mouth open wide, he'd belch and snap at the invisible vapor as it escaped. The scab ritual ended the same way every time. Bruce would position the palm of his right hand in the center of his forehead, grab the back of his head with his left hand and snap his neck with a sudden jerk. The hallways of Westmont High reverberated with the familiar sound of Bruce's cervical vertebra cracking and popping as he walked to class.

Nearly everyone was immune to Bruce's annoying eccentricities. He'd been perfecting them since grammar school. The only time they attracted attention was when a new student came to school or a substitute teacher arrived from out of the area. Bruce's revolting ritual had become as familiar to his classmates as tests on Friday or Hawaiian burgers after school. In fact, the menacing maneuver had become an integral part of Westmont culture. They created a dance in his honor called *The Bruce*. It was a venerated school tradition.

At least once at every school dance, someone would yell, "BRUCE!" That was the signal for the Bruce dance to begin. The sight of several hundred sweaty teens mimicking Bruce's hideous scab ritual—in exaggerated pantomime—was memorable, to say the least. Its amazing popularity was a product of the dramatic effect it had on the faculty chaperones who policed the school dances. It really pissed them off. They'd run around the dance floor screaming for everyone to stop, which only added to the excitement and prolonged the crowd's

crude gyrations. The lewd performance usually ended with the frantic principal turning on the lights and threatening disciplinary action.

The teachers and counselors thought that somehow Bruce's fragile psyche would be damaged by a dance that bore his name. But nothing could have been further from the truth. Bruce benefited from the notoriety in a big way. All the girls wanted to dance *The Bruce* with Bruce. For those three or four minutes he was the most popular guy in school.

He could dance with any girl at Westmont High and there was quite an impressive selection to choose from. As much as the girls vied for his attention, he always chose Beverly Hastings. Bruce was weird, but he knew a drop-dead teen goddess when he saw one. Beverly was stunning and Bruce was hopelessly in love with her.

He invited Beverly to the prom at the last minute. She already had a date and turned him down gently. Bruce took it hard. Now, he was mad at everybody. His feelings of rejection and envy ignited a fire-storm of anger that raged below the surface of his glum, yet cool exterior.

Bruce peered out the small serving window above the grill as he cooked burgers for the objects of his anger. Sweat poured from his oily forehead as he watched Beverly. She gestured excitedly and talked about the prom with her friends. An endless downpour of perspiration rained on the smoking grill. The heavy drops of sweat evaporated instantly into tiny wisps of steam. They swirled in mid-air, then disappeared up the hooded vent like angry spirits. Bruce got hotter and hotter. He slapped down crowded rows of raw beef patties on the greasy grill. The red and white disks of flattened flesh and fat couldn't seem to get comfortable on the broad black sizzling slab. Bruce felt sorry for himself and began taking out his frustrations on the docile meat. He pretended that the patties were the classmates he envied.

While his unsuspecting classmates socialized in the crowded dining area, their doubles sizzled on the smoking grill. Brad Taylor spit hot juice in Bruce's face as he mashed the handsome halfback down on the hot, hard grill. Bridget Curtis hissed as he flipped her over and plopped a slice of cheese on her bare burned back. The ever popular Jim Harper simmered passively as Bruce tormented him with his greasy metal spatula. Bruce fumed and continued to punish the ground chuck until the surrogate seniors were done. Then he slapped them down, one by one, on a tray of warm buns. He began Hawaiianizing them by adding a slice of pineapple. A fly circled overhead as the burgers endured the indignity of their tropical transformation.

When Bruce glopped bright orange sweet and sour sauce on the blackened burgers, the fly landed in the thick, sticky stuff. It struggled for a moment, then sunk silently below the surface. His first inclination was to fish it out, but he just left it there instead. The fly gave him ideas.

He muttered to himself, "Those dick-heads could use a little extra protein. I think I'll add a little something of my own."

Then he walked over to a row of square stainless steel wells that contained the condiments. He leaned forward, blocked one nostril and blew a large, loose snot-wad into the mayonnaise. It plopped down on the oily white mayo with enough force to make it jiggle. Thick amber mucus marbled the clear runny slime. Without thinking, he quickly mixed it in and moved on to the next container. Bruce hawked up a loogy and spit into the mustard. The milky, bubbling spittle settled in a shallow pool that glistened in the harsh fluorescent light.

He slopped the contaminated condiments on the burgers and arranged them on the tray. Bruce never smiled, but the corner of his mouth rose just enough to reveal his molars and gums. A sordid satisfaction swept over him as he delivered the burgers to his hungry classmates. When he got to Beverly

Hastings' table his stomach tightened in a knot. Beverly was a lovely girl. She radiated an inner beauty that rivaled her stunning outer appearance. Just looking at her made Bruce's glandular secretions go crazy. A fresh crop of zits began to erupt as he stared at her high, firm, budding breasts. He could touch them with his eyes, but not with his hands. As he stood there gawking at her unobtainable orbs, his scabby hands ached to feel their wonderful weight.

He imagined that if he could touch Beverly's miraculous mammaries—just once—he could be happy, like everyone else. Beverly looked up at him with compassion in her big bright blue eyes. She felt sorry for him as he stood there, covered with scabs, slouching in his hideous Hawaiian shirt and preposterous paper hat. Bruce leered at Beverly as he picked a seeping scab on his gangly arm. The horrible scab ritual had begun.

Beverly's soft melodic voice broke the painful silence, "Hi, Bruce. I hope I'll see you at the prom tonight. I'm sorry I couldn't go with you, but Brad invited me months ago."

Bruce could only utter a visceral grunt—his mouth was full of scabs and phlegm. He ended his repellent ritual with the customary neck snap, then turned and silently lurched back to the kitchen. He watched Beverly with morbid fascination as she ate her malicious meal.

Mr. Baxter interrupted Bruce's venomous voyeurism when he made an announcement in his West Texas drawl, "The Burger Hut is closin' early today, muchachos. We gotta rustle up a mess a He-wian burgers fer yer prom."

Baxter herded the chattering crowd of adolescents out the rickety bamboo door and locked it behind them. The rough-hewn restauranteur sauntered to the kitchen. His stiff, bowlegged gate was spryer than usual.

He pulled the catering contract out of his back pocket, unfolded it with a flourish, and read it aloud to Bruce like a royal decree, "Six hundred He-wian hamburgers to be delivered to the Elk's Lodge Reception Hall at 7:30 p.m., June 16th. Amount due upon delivery—$1,800.00."

The crusty, old Texan stuffed the crumpled document back in his pocket.

He rubbed his hands together, turned to Bruce and said, "Let's git a movin', son. There's cash in them thar burgers!"

Bruce looked puzzled, "Gee, Mr. Baxter. How are we going to make all those burgers in time? It's already 5 o'clock. It'll take at least three hours just to grind the meat!"

Mr. Baxter gestured to the back door and said, "Don't worry yersef none. Jes mosey on back here."

He led Bruce outside to a curious contraption on a flatbed trailer in the parking lot. A four foot high stainless steel cone rested on top of a mechanical maze of gears, pipes and belts. The odd assortment of industrial and automotive hardware emanated from what appeared to be a radical, muscle car motor. Its sole reason for being was to turn a giant, razor-sharp, carbide, cork-screw blade. There was little doubt that the gajillion horsepower beast was qualified for the job.

Mr. Baxter affectionately patted the imposing device and said, "Well, son, ain't she perdy? She's the biggess damn meat grinder east of the Rockies. I rented 'er over in Madison. She'll grind a whole heifer in two minutes. She's all yers, boy. The meat's in the trailer. Jes toss it in the top and watch it come out the side. That's all there is to it. I'll start 'er up fer ya. Then I gotta buy more damn buns."

A broad grin spread across the cowboy's weathered face as he kick-started the monstrous machine. Bruce jumped back from the thick exhaust and deafening roar of the engine. Leaves and dust swirled around the parking lot as Bruce loaded huge slabs of meat on a dolly. Baxter saddled up his Polynesian patterned pick-up truck, waved and drove away.

Bruce positioned a huge plastic tub under the grinder's 18

inch spout. He heaved a whole flank of beef into the cone shaped feeder. When the thick fibrous flesh hit the blades, it ground instantly to a fine pulp. Round pink ribbons of mangled meat extruded out the spout and into the huge plastic tub below.

The power and efficiency of the devilish device impressed Bruce. As he watched the ground beef fill the tub, unwholesome thoughts percolated in his seething little brain. It occurred to him that he could put anything in the machine and it would be unrecognizable when it came out. Bruce decided to add a few extra ingredients, that weren't on the menu, to his classmate's Hawaiian hamburgers.

Bruce recalled that a couple of weeks earlier, his father laid some traps for the hefty rats that rummaged around the Burger Hut at night. He searched for the traps and found a live one. A rotund rodent paced back and forth in its wood and wire prison. It was as big as a small dog and smelled foul and musky. Its coarse brown hair bristled as it bared its teeth at Bruce. He carried the trap to the grinder, opened it up and dumped the reeking rodent into the huge cone-shaped feeder. The snarling little monstrosity tried to scamper up the slippery stainless steel sides. For a moment, it seemed as if the vile beast might escape, but gravity prevailed and the rat slid into the cold steel jaws of oblivion.

A small spray of blood spattered on Bruce's Hawaiian shirt as he watched the wildly whirling blades dispatch the clawing creature in a heartbeat. He scrutinized the rat meat that oozed out the spout. It looked like hamburger to him. He went back into the kitchen and found some more traps. A dusty one below the sink caught his eye. It contained the rotting carcass of a very big and very dead rat. Ants had found it before he did. The entire surface of the vermin was a black moving mass. The head and chest cavity were entirely eaten away from the inside out. The tiny scavengers poured out the eye sockets and nostrils. The rat's taught skin and shrunken fur revealed its hollow rib cage. Bruce emptied the trap along with several others into the huge, hungry grinder and went off in search of more sickening supplements.

There were dozens of roach-motels strategically positioned all around Baxter's Burger Hut. Bruce located a fresh one behind a fifty pound sack of sugar and looked inside. There were no vacancies—it was standing room only in the cardboard bug-house. He unfolded the grimy, brown box to get a better look. A squirming bouquet of big brown bugs fanned out grotesquely as he bent the box backwards. Several impressive insects were two or three inches long. The roaches that were still alive twisted helplessly in the sticky, smelly goo that held them prisoner. Oblong egg sacks, ripped from the abdomens of fertile females as they tried to escape, littered the tacky box. Some of the eggs had hatched. Hundreds of tiny cockroaches—born to die—lay motionless in the thick gummy bait. Several of the larger specimens had enough strength to rip their own legs off in their struggle to break free. If the writhing roaches had voices, their screams would have been deafening. Bruce was his father's boy. He paused for a moment and savored the suffering of the pathetic pests, then tossed them into the grinder. He gathered up all the motels he could find and dropped them in one by one.

Bruce was running out of time. Mr. Baxter could return at any moment. He quickly added more beef to the grinder, then frantically looked around for one more contaminated component to add to the mangled meat. The dumpster near the back door caught his eye. When he lifted the heavy metal lid, a stagnant stench seared his nostrils. There were several large plastic bags full of garbage lounging in the moist muck at the bottom of the dumpster.

Bruce hoisted a dripping bag over the side. The thin, white plastic was somewhat transparent and revealed the garbage within. A few trapped flies buzzed around angrily. Bruce recognized the usual Burger Hut refuse: moldy hamburger buns, greasy mashed up French fries, green rotting meat, curdled milk in half full cartons, and a mish-mash of decaying debris. With time running short, he threw the whole bilious bag in the maniacal mechanism.

The grinder started spewing out gamey, ground garbage. Then something horrible happened. The grinder ground to a halt. Something in the garbage jammed the heavy blades. The engine strained to turn and poured out thick black smoke. The whole carnivorous contraption began to shake and shimmy violently. Bruce panicked. If the machine broke down, Mr. Baxter would discover what he'd been up to.

Without thinking, Bruce vaulted on top of the machine. He reached into the huge feeder cone and pushed down on the mound of trash to force it through. Suddenly, the razor sharp blades broke free. With a surge of unbelievable torque, the blades spun wildly. In a split second the trash was ground to bits. Bruce felt a violent tug on his arm. He yanked it out immediately, but it was too late. The merciless blades chewed his hand clean off and spit it out into the plastic tub.

For a moment there wasn't any blood or pain. He could clearly see two white, splintered bones jutting out of a red pulpy mass of meat, veins and tendons. Pale pink clumps of stringy skin dangled delicately from the mangled stump. His heart pounded hard. Blood spurted like a gusher with each beat—with the blood came the pain.

When the first wave of pain hit, it was intense. Bruce screamed and waved his bloody stump in the air. He danced around the parking lot spraying blood everywhere. He realized that if he didn't stop the bleeding, he'd be dead in a matter of minutes. He stumbled into the kitchen and looked for something to use as a tourniquet. He was woozy and afraid that he might pass out and bleed to death.

As Bruce staggered past the bubbling deep fryer, he got an idea. In a desperate bid for survival, Bruce plunged his bloody stump into the boiling oil. The searing pain was unbearable, but he let it cook for several long seconds. Then, mercifully, he blacked out. Bruce regained consciousness sprawled out on the cold concrete kitchen floor. His fricasseed forearm burned and throbbed relentlessly. The flesh was brown and blistered, but the bleeding had stopped. The deep fryer had completely cauterized the steaming stub.

Bruce stumbled to the ice machine in agony. He stuck his stump into the cold crushed ice. Instantly, a cool numbness eased the searing pain. After several minutes, he couldn't feel anything. He staggered into the restroom and opened up the first-aid kit. He smeared his stump with antibiotic ointment and swallowed a handful of aspirin with codeine. When Bruce looked in the mirror, his expression startled him. The pain and trauma had caused his mouth to freeze in a broad sardonic grin. When he tried to change his expression, he couldn't.

As Bruce's grinning face stared back him in the mirror, he heard Mr. Baxter pull up in his pick-up truck. Bruce grabbed a mop with his good hand and frantically sopped up most of the blood that was coagulating in gelatinous pools on the concrete floor. Bruce stuffed his stump in his pocket and rushed out the back door. As Baxter unloaded the burger buns from the truck, Bruce nonchalantly turned off the grinder. It sputtered and coughed, then fell silent.

Mr. Baxter looked at Bruce with a shocked expression and dropped an armful of buns. Bruce's blood ran cold. He was sure that Mr. Baxter had discovered his vile secret.

Then the old cowboy hollered, "Holy guacamole! I don't think I've ever seen you smile before. Look at you. Yer grinnin' from ear to ear. Grindin' meat mus agree with you, boy. You run along now. Have some fun at yer prom. I'll finish up here."

Bruce sighed with relief. He stumbled to his rusted-out

Buick Riviera, eased into the broken down driver's seat and drove to the prom.

When he lumbered into the Elk's Lodge, the party was well under way. He looked around and couldn't believe his eyes—everyone was so dressed up. As he slowly moved across the crowded dance floor, each person he passed smiled and said hello. Their unusually warm and friendly reaction came as a shock to Bruce.

Beverly Hastings saw him and motioned for him to join the crowd at her table. He awkwardly flopped down on a chair directly across from her. He had the urge to pick a scab, but couldn't. His scab-picking hand was no longer available. She couldn't take her eyes off him—she just kept smiling.

Finally she said, "You seem different. You're so...so...so..." She desperately searched for the right word, then blurted out, "CHEERFUL. That's it. You seem so cheerful. I don't think I've ever seen you smile before. What's up, Bruce?"

He was speechless. Burce couldn't tell her why he was grinning, so he feigned sincerity, "I guess I'm just happy to see everyone having such a wonderful time."

Beverly reached out and touched the only hand he had left, "That's sweet, Bruce. I wish you'd shown us this side of yourself sooner."

Bruce's stump began to throb again as Mr. Baxter arrived with a truck load of Hawaiian burgers.

The old cowboy spread them out over several large folding tables and called out, "Come and get 'em while they're hot."

Baxter had to jump on the stage to avoid a stampede when the crowd scrambled for the tropical burgers. Brad grabbed an armful the greasy little horrors and lugged them back to the table. Bruce turned ashen as he passed them around. When Brad handed Bruce one, he lost control of his sphincter and farted.

He nervously fanned the air and stammered, "Nnn-no th-

thanks, I already ate." Bruce winced as Beverly took a bite of her tainted hamburger, then she commented that the Hawaiian sauce tasted better than usual.

Suddenly, Beverly gasped and began to gag. Fleshy bits of muck-marbled meat flew from her contorted, yet sensual mouth and tumbled down the front of her low cut formal.

She shivered and yelped, "YUCK, I just bit down on something hard!"

Beverly delicately fished around her back molars and pulled out a mutilated graduation ring.

She wiped off the gore and read the name that was engraved inside the twisted gold band—"BRUCE FOWLER."

All eyes turned to Bruce, but he didn't notice their stunned expressions. His eyes were fixed on the meaty mess that covered Beverly's heavenly hemispheres. His jaw was slack and his eyelids fluttered uncontrollably.

Bruce's tongue aimlessly probed his twitching upper lip as a stream of bloody juice dribbled from Beverly's chin. A hot, red river of the foul fluid streamed down her neck and spilled between her cleavage. A single tear rolled down Bruce's cheek—his mangled stump throbbed in his pocket. Beverly's perfect breasts quivered timidly. Pink, pulpy morsels of meat—that were once Bruce's right hand—tenderly caressed their smooth velvety surface. Bruce finally got his hand on Beverly's boobs—but he did it the hard way.

Doctor Volmer

I hesitate to tell this tale.
It's better left unsaid.
But I must set the horror free
That squirms inside my head.

I hate to burden you this way—
My story's cruel and sad.
But if I don't tell someone soon
The truth will drive me mad.

Before I start, I caution you,
  If I may be so bold,
That when my story is complete
  It can not be untold.

I'll understand if you must leave
  Before my tale is through.
But if you're calm and curious
  I'll tell it all to you.

It seems like an eternity
  Since I was swept away
Into a twisted world of pain—
  But it was yesterday.

I marched down busy sidewalks to
  The anthem money played.
I kept time to the cadence of
  The business suit parade.

My strides were sure and confident,
  Each step a measured beat,
That pounded to the rhythm of
  A million other feet.

I had an early meeting planned
  And I was running late.
But at the time I didn't know
  That first I'd meet with fate.

I rushed toward my office fast,
  But halted in my gait.
The heel of my right wing-tip shoe
  Wedged in a metal grate.

I pulled and twisted frantically—
  My shoe would not break free.
The cold gray sidewalk would not lift
  Its rigid hold on me.

I yanked and tugged with all my strength,
  But didn't have much luck.
The more I tried to shake it loose,
  The more my foot was stuck.

My face turned red, I jerked and jumped.
  I muttered in despair.
The passersby all looked away
  As if I wasn't there.

A tattered man walked up to me.
  His face was rank and red.
He laughed and pointed at my foot,
  Then looked at me and said,

"Hey college boy, if I were you,
  Ya know what I would do?"
He winked at me and whispered low,
  "Untie the frigging shoe."

I felt too stupid and afraid
  To look him in the face.
I handed him some crumpled bills
  And loosened up the lace.

As soon as my foot wiggled free
  I staggered in retreat.
I hobbled humbly, limped and lurched
  Down 82nd Street.

The wily old man shadowed me.
  He stalked without a word—
A predator who'd singled out
  The weakest of the herd.

He tracked me like a jungle cat.
  Cold sweat soaked through my coat.
I shivered from his icy gaze.
  My heart was in my throat.

I felt his hot breath on my neck.
  The old man closed the gap.
I ambled faster down the street.
  My shoulder felt a tap.

I froze in fear, then turned around.
  The derelict was there.
He reeked of wine and rancid sweat
  And bugs crawled in his hair.

He breathed hard through his rotted teeth
And tried to catch his breath.
He was angular and bony
And had the look of death.

He said, "Hey, what's the hurry, friend?"
And spattered spit and grease.
"I almost couldn't catch you, boy.
Could this be your valise?"

He handed me my brown briefcase.
His grotesque hands were cold.
He groaned, "Could you please help me home?
My heart is weak and old."

My paranoia turned to guilt.
I walked with him awhile.
His neighborhood was less than good—
The filth and stench were vile.

A shabby storefront loomed ahead.
He crooned, "We're finally here."
The place was stark and sinister.
I tried to hide my fear.

He pointed to a faded sign
That hung above the door
And said, "I'll show you stranger things
Than you have seen before."

I shuddered as I read the sign:
  Bizarre Anomalies
The Vincent Volmer Gallery
  Of Nature's Oddities

He opened up the weathered door
  And ushered me inside.
The ominous and cluttered room
  Was dark and deep and wide.

"Permit me to present myself,"
  He said and raised his brow,
"I am Doctor Vincent Volmer."
  He grinned and took a bow.

He slipped a dingy lab coat on
  And tried to stand up tall.
His round framed tinted spectacles
  Were sinister and small.

He threw a switch and suddenly
  A flash of blinding light
Glared down on me from high above—
  The room was harsh and bright.

I looked around in disbelief,
  With horror in my eyes.
The doctor's vile collection was
  Astonishing in size.

A multitude of ghastly jars
With sickening things inside
surrounded me on creaking shelves
And leaked formaldehyde.

Colossal cases, bins and crates
With grim monstrosities
Revealed in one sad passing glance,
A thousand agonies.

Descriptive plaques were scrawled and crammed
With lewd, unwholesome text.
Each crude display I noticed was
More loathsome than the next.

At first I tried to shield my eyes,
But then I had to look.
I'd never seen such shocking freaks—
My knees got weak and shook.

The doctor clapped his hands with glee
And cried, "Come take a peek."
I peered into a dusty jar
And saw a floating freak.

"Behold the famous Duck-Bill Boy
From deep dark Katmandu.
I found the creature in the bush
In nineteen thirty two."

It was a gray and waxy thing—
So pulpy, pickled, pale.
A narrow stripe of prickly hairs
Ran down its spiny tail.

Its duck-like bill was broad and flat
With tiny pointed teeth.
Some mangy, stubby feathers grew
On top and underneath.

I saw the Inside-Out Man next,
His guts were pink and bare.
"Come look at this," the doctor said,
"It's really rather rare."

A purple curtain opened up
And Mary-Joe was there—
A stuffed, tattooed hermaphrodite
With ribbons in its hair.

He said, "If you like animals,
Here's something just for you."
I choked at the menagerie
In Volmer's mutant zoo.

He had a dog without a face,
A hairless see-through lamb,
An ossified orangutan,
A giant human clam,

A tiny pygmy elephant,
  A pregnant cyclops cat,
A multitude of reptile freaks,
  And one big boy-faced bat.

I reeled at the tremendous size
  Of Volmer's Yeti squirrel,
And sickened at the sight of his
  Albino fish-faced girl.

"Come see my prize exhibit, sir"
He squealed in dark delight.
"Now step into my private room,
It's called The Hall of Fright."

I edged into the reeking room
  Where maybe twenty-five
Repulsive mutants stared at me—
  The creatures were alive!

Some almost seemed like human beings
  With flippers, fins or claws.
One man-beast had a single horn
  And massive shark-like jaws.

A thing with pink transparent flesh
  And giant feathered plume,
Cried out in pain, then licked a wound
  And paced around the room.

As I recoiled in shock and dread,
A somber little beast
Sat up the way a puppy would
And begged to be released.

Its face looked like a human child,
Except for gills and scales.
The thing had golden silky hair
That hung in long pigtails.

When Volmer saw it talk to me
He knew it asked for help.
He dragged it to another room—
I heard it whine and yelp.

The creatures all surrounded me
And then one licked my hand.
It gazed at me with sad round eyes
And seemed to understand.

I stroked its tortured, clammy flesh
And felt a sense of dread.
The fate of those poor twisted things
Was worse than being dead.

I knew that it was time to leave—
The doctor was insane.
I did not want to be the one
To tempt his twisted brain.

The front door to The Hall of Fright
Was bolted with a key.
There were no windows in the room—
And no escape for me.

The doctor burst in from the back
With fresh blood on his coat.
He held the childlike creature tight
Around its slender throat.

He growled, "The show is over, pal!"
His voice was loud and rude.
Then Volmer asked, "What do you think
About my eerie brood?"

"It's you who are the monster here,
You should be in a cage."
And as I spoke his creatures cringed.
He flew into a rage.

He said, "You'll find out soon enough
Who is the monster here.
The world is full of oddities
And you'll be one, my dear."

He grabbed a filthy glass syringe;
It dripped with something red.
He plunged it deep into my neck;
A fire filled my head.

I could not move, I could not talk,
  But I could feel and see.
He dragged me to another room.
  I lay there helplessly.

His surgical devices laid
  In rows on filthy trays.
The scissors, saws and forceps had
  A brittle, bloody glaze.

He cleared a metal table off
  And hoisted me on top.
Then snatched a rusty scalpel up—
  I felt my buttons pop.

He leered at me with yellow teeth
  And drooled just like a fiend.
Then he began to wipe his tools—
  He chatted as he cleaned.

"I've spent my life collecting these
  Disgusting little things.
I relish the unusual—
  I love the fear it brings.

The road of evolution curves
  And detours now and then.
Mutations happen randomly—
  You don't know where or when.

When I was young I searched them out
  And gathered quite a few.
Now I'm too old to track them down.
  I thought of something new.

I was a plastic surgeon once.
  I sculpted living flesh.
Now I make my own, you see—
  My oddities are fresh.

He pinched my cheek and mussed my hair
  As he removed a sock.
Then pouted as he tweaked my toes
  And cooed in baby-talk,

"That's quite enough of me for now.
  Let's concentrate on you,
My silly little business man
  Who lost his precious shoe."

I tried to scream, but I could not,
  As Volmer went to work.
He started cutting off my suit.
  He had an evil smirk.

I heard a raucous banging sound
  Behind the bolted door.
He cursed and threw his scissors down.
  My clothes were on the floor.

The creatures in the other room
  Were grunting out his name.
The more they howled and banged away,
  The hotter he became.

He flung the huge door open wide
  And kicked his yelping spawn.
For all his violent savagery
  The freaks had not withdrawn.

Instead, the creatures drove him back
  And pinned him to the wall.
Then something bit him on the leg.
  I saw him trip and fall.

They threw him on the table top
  And scooted me aside.
He struggled hard and cried for help—
  The fiend was terrified.

His monsters ripped his lab coat off
  As pinchers, hands and claws
Snatched up the cold steel cutlery—
  They juggled knives and saws.

The doctor soiled his underpants
  As they whacked off his ears.
Their work was wicked, wild and wet
  With urine, blood and tears.

A frantic creature sawed a hand,
Another sawed a leg.
The doctor wailed and thrashed around.
The pain made Volmer beg.

They munched on raw leftover flesh
and squealed in ecstacy.
The fact that he was still alive
Seemed hideous to me.

They slashed and snipped and sewed all day—
Tenacious in their task.
By afternoon the doctor's face
Looked like a monster mask.

They rearranged his countenance;
Their work was far from neat.
A mass of muck had been sewn on
The morbid mess of meat.

The remnants of his tortured frame
Looked like a butchered boar.
Clumps of scales and feathers formed
A patchwork quilt of gore.

They modified his arms and legs
With real artistic flair.
Two tentacles replaced his arms
And pinchers clawed the air.

The doctor's paralyzing drug
  Wore off to some degree.
I scooted off the table top,
  And grabbed the deadbolt key.

I pushed the huge door open wide.
  The creatures stopped their work.
They bolted for their freedom.
  Volmer sat up with a jerk.

I heard a sickening ripping sound
  As Volmer popped his seams.
He bellowed in a gasping voice,
  "I'll see you in your dreams!"

His organs plopped into his lap.
  They quivered in a pile.
He plunged his claws into the mass
  Of entrails, blood and bile.

He stuffed his bloated stomach back
  Inside the gaping cut.
Then clutched his open abdomen
  And tried to sew it shut.

He lacked the fine dexterity
  required for the job;
So everything he'd put back in
  Just gushed out in a blob.

He muttered vile obscenities
  And fumbled with his bowels;
Then wrapped his mangled middle up
  With greasy, grimy towels.

I couldn't watch him any more.
  I screamed and hid my eyes.
He sobbed and called out to his freaks,
  But there were no replies.

I stumbled from The Hall of Fright
  And found my way out front.
I gasped a breath of outside air
  And heard a gurgling grunt.

Behind me, Volmer made his way
  Toward the open door.
In all my life, I'd never seen
  A sight like him before.

He sobbed, "Come back, my pretty pets!"
  Then chased his loathsome flock,
As several yards of viscera
  Trailed him down the block.

I stood there naked, cold and dazed,
  My briefcase in my hands;
As Volmer disappeared from sight,
  Shouting stern commands.

The doctor's frightening little friends
  had scurried off to play;
But when they heard his angry voice,
  They quickly ran away.

The creatures scattered in the street.
  Some wiggled under cars.
They slithered, crawled and scooted past
  The shops and dives and bars.

A garbage truck was passing by.
  Some monsters hitched a ride.
A freak crawled in a burned-out car
  Where it could safely hide.

A snake-like curiosity
  Climbed up a traffic light.
The light turned red, the mutant spooked
  And slithered down in fright.

A pack of hybrid canine beasts
  Pursued an alley cat.
And terrorized the patrons of
  A rundown laundromat.

An amorous anomaly
  With giant rhino balls
Was humping everything in sight
  And bumping into walls.

A twisted mound of crawling flesh
  Jumped in a garbage can.
A living sphinx snuck up and licked
  A sleeping homeless man.

I watched their grotesque silhouettes
  Against the setting sun.
The city seemed to welcome them—
  The same as everyone.

This midway made of glass and steel,
  Has always found a home
For products of a tortured mind,
  Or scrambled chromosome.

Conceived in madness, born in pain,
  These children of the knife
Explored the urban underworld
  Of downtown city life.

The gory little horrors from
  The doctor's Hall of Fright
Dissolved into the dusk and gloom,
  Then disappeared from sight.

A cool damp breeze blew from the east
  With scents from far off seas.
Musk and dander from the fur
  Of nameless oddities.

The world seemed cruel and stranger than
It did the day before.
I killed the lights in Volmer's place
And slammed the blood stained door.

I heard a distant siren wail.
The sky was turning black.
I wandered off into the night
And never did look back.

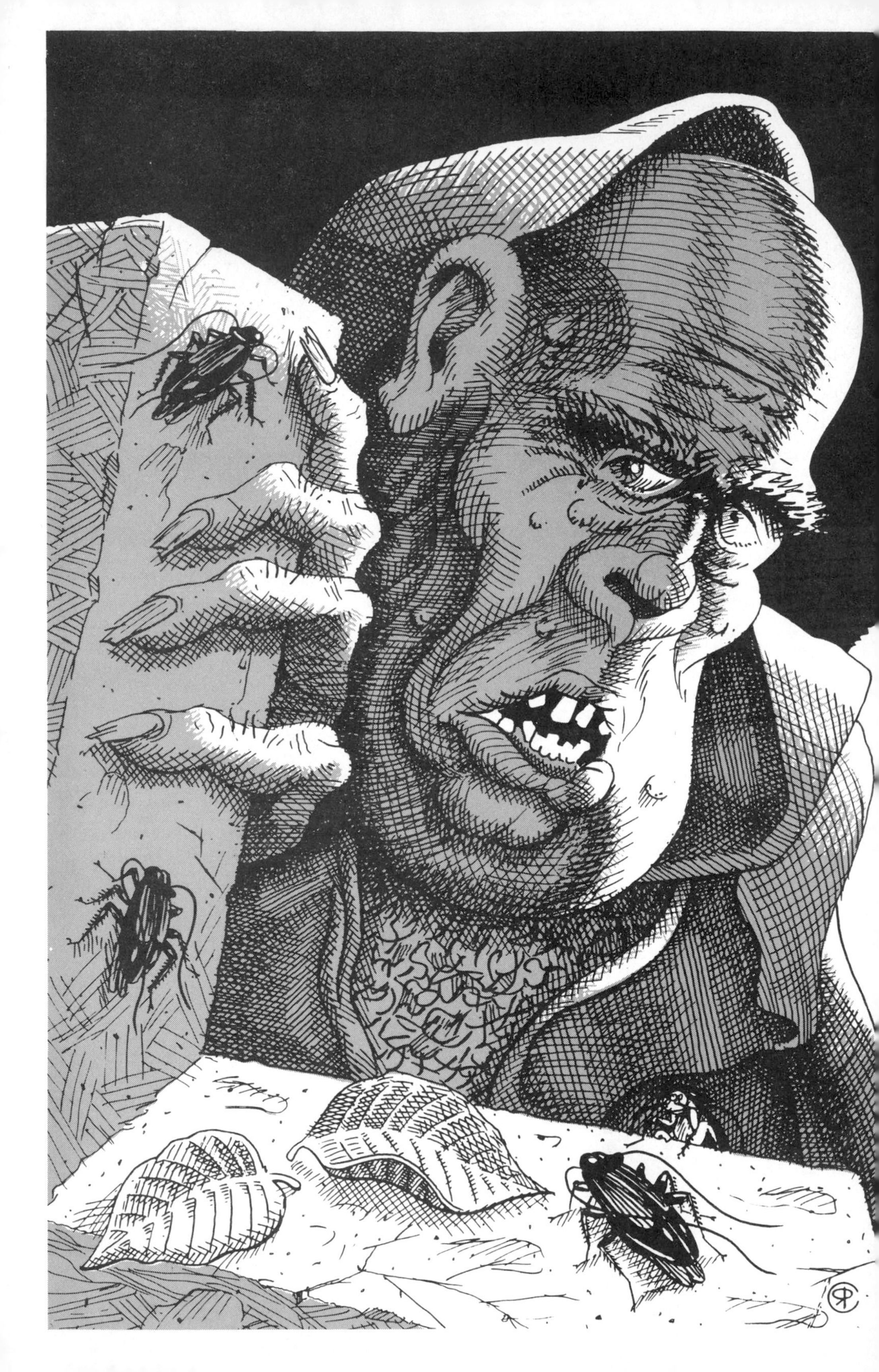

Ghouls Diet

Do you have rolls of rippling fat
  That jiggle when you walk?
Do you feel more dead than alive?
  If so, then we must talk.

If you are bloated, broad and big,
  Your energy is low.
You're not the ghoul that you once were.
  Here's something you should know:

The diet of the average ghoul
  Lacks anything that's fresh.
The only thing you ever eat
  Is decomposing flesh.

The rich and rancid rotting fat
  You gorge on every night,
Goes straight down to your hips and thighs
  And turns to cellulite.

Cut back on all the moldy meat
  You normally consume.
Control your lust for rotting flesh
  When dining in a tomb.

Just think about your arteries,
  They're hard and clogged and packed.
The horror of cholesterol
  Is now a well known fact.

You need a sensible regime
  Of food and exercise.
Your lifestyle is more dangerous
  Than you may realize.

Don't eat too much before you sleep;
  Avoid those fatty backs.
Try tender toes and finger tips—
  They're healthy bedtime snacks.

When eating your cadaver meat,
Stop half way through your meal.
Let ten or fifteen minutes pass,
Then see how full you feel.

Stay clear of feeding frenzies, fiend,
Mass burials and such.
When ghouls all get together they
Can't help but eat too much.

Watch out for those preservatives—
Avoid formaldehyde.
Try eating corpses at the morgue
Or mummies that are dried.

Were you aware that human brains
Are almost sugar-free?
They are a rich and creamy treat
That's high in energy.

You'll find all of your vitamins
Beneath the cold tombstones.
Be sure to suck the marrow out
Inside the brittle bones.

You can't drink too much lymph and bile—
That's what the experts say.
Drink body fluids when you can—
At least four quarts a day.

Try eating roughage every night—
  Some gallstones would be good.
Or maybe eat some dry grave grass,
  Or rotten coffin wood.

Devour vegetarians,
  As often as you please.
Their wholesome and organic flesh
  Is low in calories.

The vital role of exercise
  Can not be stressed enough.
Most ghouls are really out of shape
  And not especially tough.

You ghouls just lounge around the crypt,
  Then eat your dinner late.
You lack a sense of discipline,
  And never watch your weight.

Jog three time 'round the old graveyard
Before you start to eat,
You'll find it helps you to digest
The sweet decaying meat.

Don't be afraid to break a sweat,
You're not an invalid!
Before you eat your coffin meat,
Do pushups on the lid.

Just use a little common sense,
And learn these simple rules.
There's nothing more disgusting than
A bunch of flabby ghouls.

MIGNOLA
94

Slime Soup

RANDY'S annual *Summer and Gommorrah* party was a benchmark in Labor Day weekend debauchery. Most of his co-workers from the real estate office were already grazing on mixed nuts as Randy dried his hair with one hand and juggled a platter of exotic cheese with the other. No one dared miss a single wicked minute of the infamous celebration. Detailed accounts of past excesses and outrageous indiscretions were now legend among house-traders from Pacific Palisades to Hancock Park. Randy's party was more important to the raucous realtors than a new listing. The sales-hungry predators were quarrelsome and competitive, as usual, but the grinding drone of Margaritas in the blender drowned out their habitual bickering. As the evening progressed, their constant chiding eventually turned into glandular party patter.

This year's gala was definitely Randy's hottest blow-out ever—the air conditioning in his luxurious, high-tech condo was broken. The triple digit temperature put a sweaty, Tennessee Williams, spin on the evening. The oddly amorous combination of perspiration and alcohol led to such unexpected pairings that no one would be immune to ridicule—come Tuesday morning. Randy was no exception.

Early in the evening, he made an ardent offer to Irene Spencer that she put into escrow before the guacamole turned

brown. It must have been the heat, because ordinarily the only thing that could get a rise out of *The Czarina of Brentwood* was a foreclosure. Randy and Irene melted into the sofa and swapped spit until the party started breaking up around 2:00 a.m.

Randy was eager to keep Irene's motor running. He killed the lights, ushered the stragglers out the door and locked up in record time. Randy and Irene drove to her hedonistic habitat at the beach and spent the next two days consummating their infatuation. By Labor Day morning, the party was definitely over. They reverted to their normal combative relationship and argued over runny eggs, until Randy awkwardly excused himself and drove home.

The air was hot and soggy as he guided his key into the front door dead-bolt. As the cylinder rotated and the bolt snapped open, he remembered that he'd left in such a hurry that he hadn't cleaned up after the party. The thought of the mess that awaited him—after three days of oppressive heat—made him wish that he was still arguing with Irene in her breezy beach house. He braced himself, wiped the sweat from his forehead, and opened the door just enough to survey the damage. A foul smelling blast of moist heat and flies forced its way through the slender crack as the door inched open. The acrid aroma seared Randy's nostrils and triggered an instant gag reflex.

He reeled backwards choking in disgust and steadied himself on the wrought-iron porch railing until his head stopped spinning. Randy had never been squeamish and he didn't intend to start now. In fact, he always had a morbid fascination for the gross and grotesque. After his initial shock had worn off, he seemed to relish the opportunity to confront the monstrous mess that waited for him.

Randy braced himself, held his nose and flung the door open wide. His eyes filled with tears as noxious fumes belched from his corrupted condo. A profound sense of amazement overpowered his initial feeling of disgust as he gazed in wonder at the horror that loomed before him. The degree to which the usual party fare had degenerated in just two days took him totally by surprise. He expected a certain amount of decay, with the heat and all, but nothing like the sickening scene that assaulted his senses. Cleaning a mess of that magnitude required a strategic plan.

He thought for a moment, then rushed downstairs and grabbed a large galvanized metal bucket from the laundry room. When he returned to the ominous entrance of his once pristine home, bewildered neighbors hovered around his front door. The inquisitive group held their noses, timidly peeked inside, then cautiously stepped back. They whispered to one another and speculated that their young neighbor must be dead inside. The bilious bystanders sighed with relief when Randy pushed his way through the crowd. He assured everyone that calling the police was totally unnecessary and encouraged them to return to their homes. They shuffled off in a mild state of shock. Randy forced a smile and thanked them for their concern as he mechanically waved good-bye.

With bucket in hand, he crossed the threshold with grim determination. Once inside, Randy surveyed his sordid living room. He approached the mess with the curiosity and enthusiasm of an anthropologist. He felt as if he had stumbled upon the site of some barbaric, yet fascinating ritual. The reeking relics of his famous summer gala surrounded him in a vista of vile disintegration. The individual components of the dreadful debris decomposed at their own pace. At first it was difficult to identify the contents of the countless bowls and platters that littered the living room. A closer inspection revealed undeniable evidence that a grotesque metamorphosis had occurred.

On one platter, guacamole had transformed into what appeared to be bean dip with a shock of wispy, white hair.

Behind the sofa, someone knocked over a fondue pot into a large overflowing ashtray. The unexpected combination of ingredients looked like a grayish-purple alien landscape—complete with unfamiliar flora and fauna. Other mutations were less picturesque and more repulsive. Several roguish anchovy cheese rolls seemed to have mated with some rotten deviled eggs. The unwholesome union spawned what appeared to be blue caviar in a clear viscous sludge. The spiced cabbage mounds had taken on a life of their own. Broken bits of gourmet crackers jutted up from what remained of the salmon mousse. They looked like crooked teeth protruding from sickly pink gums. The misshapen mouth grinned up at Randy and mocked his hopes of bringing order to the chaos he had created. The effect that time and temperature had on the stuffed beets was so lewd that Randy simply winced and looked away. He never realized the variety of household pests that shared his condo with him. The scummy residue in several clear plastic cups contained a better collection of bugs than most natural history museums. The laughter and the music were gone now—all that remained was decay.

Randy began dumping the rancid remnants of his party into the eager emptiness of the giant metal bucket. As the warm flat beer and skunky wine mingled with milky glazed shrimp aspic, curdled brown onion dip and old cigarette butts, he remembered a game from his grammar school days. He and his best friends, Arty and Ben, would sneak into his mother's kitchen. They filled the tallest glass they could find with mustard, Tabasco sauce, pepper and whatever unappetizing ingredients they could scavenge from the backs of cabinets and the bottoms of drawers. They called their concoction *Slime Soup*. The one who could taste the unsavory soup, without gagging, was the winner. Randy always won and earned the coveted title *Mr. U. R. Gross*. He thought to himself, "I wonder if Mr. U. R. Gross could taste *this* slime without getting sick?" He laughed maniacally and continued filling the bucket.

As Randy added more ingredients to the hideous concoction, his mind began to wander. He fancied himself as Monsieur U.R. Gross, master chef of filth. With a sudden flair, he flung bluish ham slices and moist, moldy chips into the hungry bucket. He muttered to himself in a French accent and fantasized that he was the host of a TV cooking show. He proceeded to teach an imaginary audience how to make Slime Soup at home: "First you get zee bucket, zen you add zome rotten feelth. Pour in a leetle moldy wine, spreenkle with ceegerette ashes and voila—Zlime Zoop! Bon appètit!"

The more nauseating the mixture became, the more a strange compulsion to sample the loathsome soup dominated his thoughts. "What if I really did it? What if I actually ate some of this slop?" He tried to drive the thought from his mind by thinking about his weekend marathon with Irene Spencer. But the desperate drive festered in the back of his mind. He was starting to feel a little squeamish as he added milky brown tuna and pungent goose liver pate to the putrid pail. It was almost full when he reached the entrance of the kitchen.

The kitchen doorway framed a vision of such pernicious pestilence that Randy lurched backwards in mute repulsion. The kitchen counter was alive with a writhing blanket of squirming maggots. The legless larvae had hatched inside the decomposing remains of several uneaten Cornish game hens. The putrid little birds still waited patiently to be served on their sterling silver platter. The oily skin of the infested fowl rippled as the parasites feasted on the fetid flesh within.

Beyond the tiny rotting carcasses was a row of half-full wine bottles—of questionable vintage. Beyond that, a plain translucent plastic bowl loomed menacingly on the cluttered kitchen counter. The color drained from Randy's face and his knees buckled as he remembered what the bowl contained.

Randy had a reputation as a gourmet with his friends, and he delighted in serving his guests savory and unexpected taste treats. That's why he always insisted on using only fresh clams in his famous seafood dip. The lidded bowl contained the shelled clams that didn't make it into the dip. An ominous condensation on the air-tight lid was proof that the clams were anything but fresh. Randy inched his way toward the bowl. His hands trembled as he reached for it. A battle raged inside his mind. Logic told him to leave it alone, but Mr. U. R. Gross wanted to look inside. For an instant he almost came to his senses and threw the wretched thing into the trash, but his dark obsession drove him on.

He toyed with the bulging bowl as he tried to decide if he should remove the sealed lid. It was bowing up under considerable internal pressure as he explored its smooth, warm surface with his twitching fingers. He realized that what he now held in his hands was the missing ingredient that would make his caustic concoction complete. He whispered, "If only Ben and Arty were here now to behold the ultimate Slime Soup."

Without further deliberation, he began to pry open the lid. There was a faint hissing sound, then a loud pop as the lid ricocheted off the kitchen ceiling. An unbearably foul stench seared his nostrils and sent an olfactory overload to his brain. It exploded with a shock wave of nausea that triggered an upheaval so violent that he couldn't breathe. His bladder emptied uncontrollably as he gasped for breath. Randy's eyes bulged and locked onto the contents of the ghastly plastic bowl. He tried to look away, but could not.

The putrefying clams huddled together in yellowish-gray gelatinous blobs. Tiny white colonies of virulent bacteria speckled the dull wet surface of the decomposing mollusks. Randy's quivering hands made the clams seem almost alive as they jiggled at the bottom of the slimy bowl. As he fought for air, the bowl slipped from his hands. The festering contents of

the loathsome plastic vessel spilled into the bucket of gurgling goo in a series of limp plops. Randy began to catch his breath. At first he could only manage small gulps of air. Then in one giant gasp, he filled his lungs to capacity. His throat and chest burned from the pungent fumes that filled the room.

Randy sat on the floor with his legs crossed and panted like a sick puppy. He positioned the sloshing bucket of frothing filth between his knees. His head throbbed as he mindlessly rocked back and forth. Dazed and disoriented, he stared into the bucket and watched the Slime Soup slop back and forth. Randy was mesmerized by the fluid movement and subtle currents within the bucket. The dissimilar viscosities and horrible hues of the various squalid liquids created nauseating swirls of runny greens and creamy ochres. The tainted flotsam and jetsam of Randy's party bobbed on the surface of the malignant mixture. He calmly watched the obscene chunks of scum twist and turn in the sloshing bucket of filth. Then he noticed that the prime ingredient was missing.

In a panic, he bellowed, "WHERE ARE THE CLAMS?"

Without hesitation, he rolled up his sleeve and plunged his hand deep into the percolating slime. He shuttered in disgust as the warm sludge oozed between his fingers. He kneaded the dense, lumpy sediment at the bottom of the bucket until he felt something smooth and meaty.

"GOTCHA!"

Randy raised a plump, slippery clam high above his head. Thick rancid slime slowly ran down his arm. Globs of coagulated gunk dripped onto his face and hair as he admired his unwholesome prize. His eyes twitched with anticipation as he brought the loathsome thing close to his lips.

The timid monstrosity seemed to shiver with excitement as he crooned, "There you are, my pretty!" He tenderly petted the muck drenched mollusk and continued, "Could you possibly taste as good as you look?"

Randy moistened his lips and licked the caustic clam with one long, slow slurp. Its pungent taste made him wince, but nothing could stop him now. He threw his head back like a sword swallower, popped it into his mouth, and swallowed the monstrous thing whole.

The corpulent clam slithered down Randy's gullet like a bloated slug. When it finally wiggled into his stomach, his abdominal muscles tightened. A sharp, burning pain gripped his belly. Randy's stomach didn't share his enthusiasm for Slime Soup—he doubled over in agony and dropped to his knees.

A wave of intense nausea swept over him. His spine became rigid. In one violent surge he vomited the fleshy blob with such force that it projected across the kitchen and plopped down in the middle of the living room floor. Randy whimpered and collapsed face down in a frothing puddle of his own puke. He used what little strength he had left to raise his head. It was enough to track the trajectory of the clam.

His eyes followed a trail of vomit that led to the soggy regurgitated creature. It lay motionless in a viscus pool of foul smelling bile and digestive juices—between a pair of elegant women's shoes. As Randy looked up, he realized that the petite feet in the white Italian pumps were attached to Irene Spencer's well worked-out legs. She stood speechless, a vision of loveliness in her white blouse and crisply pleated navy blue Chanel skirt. She had dropped by to make up with Randy and arrived just in time to witness the entire interchange between her Labor Day lover and his cadaverous clam.

If humiliation was lethal, Randy would have dropped dead on the spot. He was so mortified that he hid his face in his hands and sobbed uncontrollably. In a pathetic attempt to recover his dignity, he smoothed back his matted, filth clotted hair and wiped some of the muck off his clothes. After a few moments of pathetic preening, he found the courage to look at Irene. The expression on her radiant, well-scrubbed face made

Randy feel like a lower life form. He shrank from the startled, questioning look in her eyes. He shrank even smaller when she stared into his hideous bucket.

Suddenly, Irene's horrified expression turned to one of recognition. A sly knowing look spread across her face and she started to laugh.

Then in a playground voice, she shouted; "Slime Soup! You bad boy! I know what you've been up to. I used to make the worst Slime Soup in my neighborhood—and I could eat it too. Nothing could gross me out."

A sheepish smile lit up Randy's grimy face. He shook his head in disbelief and crawled toward her.

Irene helped him to his feet and said, "I must admit you're not bad for an amateur."

Then with a crafty smile, she pointed to the bucket and asked, "What's a girl have to do to get something to eat around here?"

Uptown Ribs

To say that I love barbecue
  Would understate the fact
That when it comes to ribs and links,
  My tastes are quite exact.

They must be meaty, not too lean,
  With sauce that's hot and thick.
I like them smoky, cooked real slow
  In pits made out of brick.

I've had a thing for barbecue
  As long as I recall.
Hot links, sliced beef, pork ribs or tips—
  I'm crazy for them all.

I'm healthy, but I weigh too much,
  By twenty pounds or so.
But I gave up on dieting
  A year or two ago.

I know that it's not popular
  To speak of barbeque.
But I'm a man of simple tastes—
  Please hear my story through.

I am a cop—Detective Nash—
  And I've seen pain and gore.
If barbeque seems gross to you,
  I will not tell you more.

But if you have an appetite
  For raw and juicy tales,
I have a graphic anecdote,
  I know will curl your nails.

Back when I was a rookie cop
  I had an attitude.
My partner taught me to survive—
  And where to go for food.

My first day out he took me to
A rib joint on Vermont.
The homey hut had everything
A carnivore could want.

In those days they used hickory
To smoke the slabs of meat.
We smelled those ribs a block away,
As we patrolled the street.

The first time I sat down to eat
Inside that stucco shack,
My partner called to Byron and
He came in from the back.

I ordered links and rare beef ribs
With extra sauce and beans,
A giant wedge of hot corn bread
And lots of collard greens.

That barbeque was so superb
That I came back again.
In fact, I think I've eaten there
Most every day since then.

The joint is called The Old Brick Pit,
Back then it had no name.
It's owned by Byron Lomax and
He's kept the food the same.

We've been good friends for so long now,
His quirks make sense to me.
He's always worn a red beret.
And bristly, black goatee.

He has a patch on his right eye,
He's big and mean and strong.
He boxes with the younger guys—
Sometimes I tag along.

A while ago a hopped-up punk
Was tearing up his place.
So Byron threw him on the grill
And barbequed his face.

The wiseguy's friends came back that night
With blackjacks and a gun.
When Byron grabbed his butcher knife,
You should have seen them run.

He sliced this one guy's fingers off
As he ran through the door.
They flew behind the counter
And rolled across the floor.

I grabbed the punk and cuffed him to
A heavy metal chair.
Then gathered all his fingers up—
The blood was everywhere.

This guy who seemed a real hard case,
  Cried like a little kid.
He waved his stubby hand and sobbed
  "Look what that asshole did."

I put his severed fingers in
  A plastic bag with ice
And drove him to emergency.
  I gave him some advice.

I said, "If you think this is bad,
  You'd better think again.
I've seen my friend do far worse things
  To much, much tougher men.

So stay away from Byron's place.
  And tell your little friends
That next time they might get a load
  Of lead in their rear ends."

The sniveling tough guy never heard
  A single word I said.
He'd passed out cold on my back seat—
  He looked like he was dead.

When we got to the hospital
  They pulled him from the back
And took him to the E.R. with
  His gory little sack.

I know they put his fingers back—
  At least to some degree.
I saw him once in Echo Park.
  He flipped the bone at me.

When Byron gets a little hot,
  I try to cool him down.
He's always been a friend to me
  And every cop in town.

His business really took a dive
  A year or two ago.
But lately it's been really good—
  It's hardly ever slow.

Cholesterol-a-phobics had
  Stopped eating barbecue.
But then some gourmet magazine
  Gave him a rave review.

Now Byron's place is always packed.
  It's busy and it's loud.
Some nights he brings a combo in
  To entertain the crowd.

I passed on lunch last Saturday,
  And worked till three o'clock.
A call came on the radio.
  I drove to Eagle Rock.

Another severed head turned up—
This one was far from fresh.
I couldn't find a drop of blood,
Or any other flesh.

Some kids had found it near a gym—
Inside a canvas bag.
And when I pulled the zipper back
The odor made me gag.

Its dry, wide eyes stared up at me.
Its skin was white as chalk.
The way the mouth was open wide,
Looked like the head could talk.

The victim was an adult male—
Caucasian, twenty-five.
His shocked expression was so real,
The head seemed half alive.

It had a yellow sweat band on
And headphones still in place.
If this guy had been jogging late,
He didn't win the race.

I closed the bag and called downtown.
This grizzly murder spree
Had gone unsolved for seven months.
It really got to me.

Some sick, sadistic psychopath,
  Or a hatchet-happy kook,
Had filled the morgue with body parts.
  It made me want to puke.

We now had forty severed heads
  And piles of hands and feet.
But not one body had been found.
  The Mayor was taking heat.

A leg bone turned up in the trash
  On Sunset Boulevard.
The skin and flesh had been removed
  With something sharp and hard.

The sticky femur was a mass
  Of ants and coffee grounds
That rolled off when I pulled it from
  The putrid moving mounds.

The Medical Examiner
  Explored the bone with glee.
He poked and picked the loathsome thing,
  Then turned and grinned at me.

He pointed to some jagged marks
  And yelled, "ELECTRIC KNIFE!
They always leave these kind of grooves—
  I bought one for my wife.

I also found a plastic chip."
He probed a meaty shred,
Then raised his tweezers to the light—
The tiny chip was red.

He looked at it from every side
And said, "You have a choice,
It's from a broken tail light lens—
A Jaguar or Rolls Royce."

At last, we finally had a lead—
The only one so far.
Our killer had to be someone
Who owned a fancy car.

I drove back to The Old Brick Pit;
The lunch crowd had all gone.
A blue Rolls Royce was parked out front.
Its engine was still on.

It was a risky thing to do.
The trunk was open wide
The driver's window was rolled down
And no one was inside.

The Old Brick Pit was empty now—
As quiet as a tomb.
But I could smell fresh barbeque
As I surveyed the room.

When Byron came out from the back
He walked out with a man—
Armani suit, a Rolex watch,
Too hip and way too tan.

They carried metal serving plates
With high, clear plastic tops.
The mounds of steaming barbecue
Dripped greasy little drops.

There must have been a hundred pounds
Of sliced meat, ribs and links.
They filled the rear seat of the Rolls,
Then got some beans and drinks.

They juggled boxes, beer and bags.
I helped and took a few.
I slammed the Roller's trunk down hard
And something hit my shoe.

When I looked down the things I saw
Were shiny, red and bright—
The broken bits of plastic from
A busted-up tail light!

I waved to Byron and his friend
And said I couldn't stay.
Then jumped into my unmarked car.
The Roller pulled away.

He headed west on Sunset fast,
Drove through the Bel-Air gate,
Then snaked around the hills awhile.
I checked his license plate.

The car belonged to Donald Smote.
His record came up blank.
No wants or warrants, he was clean—
A bigwig at a bank.

He turned right on a private road.
His yard looked like a park.
Huge iron gates flew open wide.
I heard some guard dogs bark.

Smote parked his car and popped the trunk.
I stayed back on the street.
The house looked like a French chateau.
His maid hauled in the meat.

The sun hung low behind a hill
As cars pulled up the drive.
The soft light gleamed on chrome and paint.
I watched the guests arrive.

A grand procession passed by me—
Stretch limos, jewels and clothes.
I recognized a face or two
From films and TV shows.

It seemed almost impossible
  The murderer was there.
Could such a savage killer be
  A well known millionaire?

I had to find some answers fast.
  I went to Byron's place.
I found him counting out his cash.
  A smile was on his face.

I asked "Who is this Donald Smote?"
  He beamed at me and said,
"He's one of my best customers,
  He's got a lot of bread.

He runs a ritzy gourmet club—
  They really like to eat.
When I was broke and in the dumps,
  They got me on my feet.

They have a dinner once a week—
  A sumptuous affair.
They're called The Epicureans.
  They all live in Bel-Air.

They come here every Friday night—
  They like my barbecue.
But they are real particular.
  Here's what they have me do:

They tell me when they're coming in
  And make me clear the pit.
They want their order cooked alone.
  It's quirky, I admit.

They pay me several hundred bucks,
  In cash, when I begin.
It really works out good for me—
  They bring their own meat in!

When all the meat is cooked and cut,
  They take what looks the best.
They always leave a lot behind,
  So I just sell the rest."

He pointed to the menu board,
  "Up there next to the tips—
It's called the Uptown Special, Clark."
  Then Byron licked his lips.

I hadn't eaten all day long—
  It sounded good to me.
He brought a plate of plump short ribs,
  I moaned in ecstasy.

The ribs were tender, sweet and lean.
  The meat fell off the bone.
I've had a lot of barbecue,
  But those ribs stood alone.

I savored every single bite
  And then I ordered more.
I hadn't eaten anything
  As good as that before.

The ribs were plump and succulent
  And moist beyond belief.
I turned to Byron and I asked,
  "Are these ribs pork or beef?"

He shook his head and then he said,
  "I honestly can't say.
I asked one of those gourmet guys
  The same thing just today.

The kind of meat they bring to me
  Is not a meat I've seen.
It's nicely marbled, firm and fresh—
  It's oily, but it's lean.

When I cut through the deep red ribs,
  They're stringier than pork;
And bloodier than lamb or beef
  When I stick in my fork."

I said, "I have a good idea,
  I'll take some ribs downtown.
We'll let the lab-boys sort it out.
  I bet they'll run it down."

I took a bag of Uptown Ribs
To Doctor Eddy Cooke.
His lab was always open late.
He said he'd take a look.

The bag was brown and soaked with grease.
I held it tenderly.
He said, "These ribs look dangerous,
You'd better cover me."

He grabbed a rib and sniffed the sauce,
Then winked and put it back.
He licked his fingers, smiled and said,
"They're kangaroo or yak."

I said, "Hey Eddy, knock it off,
I really want to know."
He laughed and took a closer look,
Then frowned and mumbled low,

"I don't find this amusing, Clark.
Is this some kind of joke?
This damn thing is a human rib."
Then I began to choke.

I felt a violent spasm grip
The middle of my gut.
I threw up with a frantic heave
And fell back on my butt.

He dodged my first barrage of barf—
The next one hit him square.
The half digested human flesh
Engulfed his face and hair.

The ghastly globs of gurgling goo
Were streaked with brown and red.
The murder victims' faces spun
around inside my head.

Poor Eddy stood there in a daze,
Too shocked to even speak.
I stumbled to a metal sink
my legs felt numb and weak.

I belched and moaned and retched some more
Until my heaves were dry.
I turned to Eddy, shook my head,
Then coughed and said goodbye.

I staggered slowly to my car,
And drove back to Bel-Air.
The party was still going strong,
And all the guests were there.

I snuck back to the kitchen door,
And quickly ducked inside.
The gourmet ghouls were dining late.
I found a place to hide.

I peered into the dining room
  And watched their frightful feast.
I cringed each time they sunk their teeth
  Into the cooked deceased.

The way they chewed was horrible
  They gnawed away with lust.
And when they swallowed, I recoiled
  And shivered in disgust.

They talked and ate and passed a plate
  Piled high with human gore.
Their bloated bellies swelled with flesh
  And still they wanted more.

A buffed-out matron munched a rib;
  And as she chewed she sighed.
When asked why she had joined the club
  The socialite replied,

"Sex and drugs and charities,
  Have all become a bore.
I dabbled at collecting art,
  But yearned for something more."

A balding foreign diplomat
  With brown spots on his head
Was somewhat philosophical.
  He drooled and then he said,

"When you can have most anything,
It's hard to buy a thrill,
But once you taste forbidden fruit,
You want to eat your fill."

A nervous guy with long blond hair
displayed a snotty sneer
As he caressed a fleshy link.
He spoke precise and clear,

"I'm known in every restaurant,
From here to Malibu,
Nouvelle cuisine is tres passé.
Please pass the barbecue."

I recognized a movie star—
A beautiful brunette.
As blood and sauce ran down her cheek
She spoke with deep regret,

"I'm sad for all the animals,
And forests in Brazil.
It seems like only human beings
Are still okay to kill."

A man in cowboy boots and hat
Held up a well-picked bone.
He waved it at the actress as
He spoke up with a groan,

"I don't care much for politics,
I'm interested in taste.
Just slide those short ribs over here,
Before they go to waste."

Then Smote stood up and tapped his glass,
"Attention everyone,
We have some business to discuss
Before our dinner's done.

Next week it will be Rita's turn
To bring the sweet red meat.
I'd like a few suggestions please?
What would you like to eat?"

"Let's have Italian," someone said.
Another crooned, "Chinese."
A bald man yelled, "No, make it French,
Or maybe Japanese!"

Smote turned to Rita and he said,
"Let's go for something new,
We've never eaten Japanese—
You'd better bring us two."

With that, I'd really heard enough,
So I burst through the door,
They laughed as I arrested them,
Their mouths were full of gore.

An old witch in an evening gown,
  Poked me from behind.
The snooty woman held her nose,
  Then glared at me and whined,

"You are a crude disgusting man—
  A noxious smelling brute.
You spoiled my fragile appetite
  With vomit on your suit."

I said, "Okay, you cannibal,
  Get up against the wall."
She just kept gorging human flesh,
  And didn't move at all.

Then Donald Smote looked up and said
  "Now take it easy, sir.
We still have other options left
  I'm sure you will prefer.

How does a million dollars sound?
  Would that help you forget?"
I said, "You'll need much more than cash
  To pay your bloody debt."

He lunged and grabbed a carving knife.
  I pulled my thirty-eight
And shot the slimeball in the head—
  His face went in his plate.

A chunk of skull had blown clean off.
His brains flew in the air.
The actress caught a slimy clump
And fell down off her chair.

A pale gray pulpy blob of brain
Dripped down her low cut gown.
She screamed and tried to wipe it off,
And madly hopped around.

A Nordic, buzz-cut muscle man
Jumped up and grabbed my shirt.
I put a little round, red hole
Where I knew it would hurt.

His girlfriend grabbed a serving fork
So I gave her one too.
But she kept coming after me,
And tried to run me through.

She missed me when I stepped aside
And skewered a well dressed man.
The fork was buried in his chest,
But he got up and ran.

The other guests had seen enough,
They didn't want to play.
I called downtown for back-up.
And led the ghouls away.

A swarm of squad cars swept across
  The lawn of the estate.
The suspects burped and farted from
  The morbid meal they ate.

Their mouths and hands were clotted with
  Coagulated sauce.
I cuffed them tight and lined them up
  And gave them to my boss.

The Captain looked them up and down,
  He shook his head and sighed,
"Take all these psycho-socialites
  Downtown to Homicide."

I drove back down to Byron's place,
  Well after closing time.
I found him cleaning out the pit.
  I watched him scrape the grime.

I poured a cup of coffee dregs.
He said, "How 'bout some food?
There's still some Uptown Special left."
I tried not to be rude.

"Those ribs are evidence," I said,
"There's been a gruesome crime.
We'll talk about it soon enough,
But now is not the time.

I've had my fill of barbecue;
I need a substitute.
By any chance, could you bring me
Some cottage cheese and fruit?"

Family Dinner

MARGO Woodbury gazed restlessly out the window of her father's sleek corporate chopper as it carried her home. She watched its undulating shadow creep across the Connecticut countryside like a colossal insect. A glint of sunlight broke her concentration and she shifted her attention to her reflection in the tinted glass. The bored expression that glanced back at her had taken generations of practice and breeding to perfect. Her aristocratically raised brow and heavy eyelids were usually sufficient to mask her real feelings. But today, a trace of agitation showed through her regal smirk.

Perhaps it was because her underpants had been riding up her butt crack since she left Rhode Island. Or maybe it was her Uncle Hilton's unexpected demise. She was sad, death always annoyed her. Her uncle's untimely passing interrupted her anthropology research. In the two years that she'd been away at college, this was the third time that she had to rush home to attend a family funeral.

The Woodbury clan substituted propriety for closeness. Funeral attendance topped their list of social obligations. Margo was not rebellious and always dutifully complied. The funerary ritual signaled the transfer of wealth and power—that made it the most popular spectator sport in Garien.

Margo hated funerals, but she loved the clothes. She

looked stunning in black. Uncle Hilton was not one of her favorite relatives. Actually none of her relatives were anyone's favorite anything. Hilton Woodbury never married and would surely leave his portion of the family fortune to her father. As always, Margo would exhibit the appropriate degree of grief. At the moment, her underpants gave her enough grief for several funerals. She squirmed in her seat and tried to adjust her peevish panties.

She enjoyed these solitary helicopter rides. They gave her a break from the voices in her head. Ever since she was three years old, she could hear what other people were thinking. Not everything—just the thoughts that directly related to her. It started with her mother. Margo answered her questions before she could ask them. Margo knew that it upset her mother, so she learned to hide her telepathic talent.

As Margo grew older, she began to hear what everyone was thinking. When she was little, it was more of a curse than a blessing. More than once, she cried herself to sleep over a cruel or cutting thought that found words inside her mind. Now that she was older she couldn't imagine life without her extra sense. She regarded everyone else's mind-blindness as a handicap and wondered how regular people could tell who their friends were—or what a stranger's true intentions might be. When she started having sex, the erotic ramifications of her gift became apparent. She discovered that she was able to experience her partner's excitement as well as her own. Unfortunately, her experiments in telepathic ecstasy were too brief to be conclusive. Two pimple-faced prepsters and one smooth talking professor—all prone to premature ejaculation—were all she had to go on. Margo could hear the pilot wonder if she had fallen asleep.

The rhythmic drone of the chopper's engine and steady cadence of the whirling blades usually lulled her to sleep, but this time she was too fatigued to doze off. She was one all-

nighter and one cup of coffee over the line. Her cultural anthropology term paper was due in three days. All she had was a rough outline and the title—*"The Institution of Cannibalism: A Survey of the Practice in Primitive and Developed Societies."*

The Asmat tribe from the Sepic River region of New Guinea was the focus of her research. She'd struggled all night to determine if their complex and convoluted kinship system had any bearing on their cannibalism. In the '60s they were famous for fifteen minutes when they had the audacity to eat one of the American aristocracy's favorite sons. No one had informed the bright young anthropologist that his position at the top of the food chain was up for grabs as soon as he left the continental United States.

The thought of a Woodbury on the menu in some buggy Third World jungle made Margo laugh. The Woodburys weren't the outdoors type. Her father's idea of going native was a long weekend at Palm Beach or eating Thai food with chop sticks in Manhattan. Margo was different. She couldn't wait to go into the field and use her special gift to gain new insights into the tribal mind.

Margo began to ponder the mysteries of cannibalism as she darted toward Garien at 250 miles per hour. It was a subject that had fascinated her since childhood. When she was nine, she read an article in the Reader's Digest. It was about an airliner that crashed in the Andes Mountains in Chile. One of the survivors gave a first hand account of their grisly fight for survival. In the end, they all wound up eating the frozen flesh of their family and friends who perished in the crash. Margo reread the gory parts over and over.

The survivors were all devout Catholics. The story explained how they overcame their initial squeamishness by reverently likening their cannibalism with the sacrament of Holy Communion. The analogy was not as obvious to little Margo as it was to the crash survivors. Her lessons at Sunday school had not prepared her for the more gruesome aspects of her faith. She fidgeted in her plush leather seat as she recalled her childhood obsession with the religious riddle. Margo remembered trying to unravel the mystery, but no great truth was revealed. The more she thought about it, the less sense it made.

In desperation, she went to Reverend Aldridge for guidance. She usually stayed clear of the Reverend because his breath smelled like alcohol and his thoughts scared her. His mind was always full of images of women from the church. They were naked and the Reverend did scary things to them. The Reverend was no theological visionary, but he was the only source of spiritual guidance that Garien had to offer.

Reluctantly, Margo took her chances and told him about her revelation. Like generations of Clergyman before him, the Reverend was not in the market for any new ideas. At first he was dumfounded. Then anger quickly replaced his shock. The Reverend's hostile thoughts confused Margo. A storm of contradictions and paradoxes raged in his mind. When Margo pressed him for the answer to the riddle, he put his hands on his hips and glared at her. His face turned red and the veins at his temples pulsed with religious rage.

Margo watched from the chopper's window as a large black crow disappeared into a heart shaped cloud. Her bones rattled from the vibrating helicopter as she remembered the Reverend's reply. He lifted little Margo off the ground like a doll and shook her with the zeal of an inquisitor. He accused her of everything from blasphemy to necromancy.

He shook and shouted until he tired himself out. When his anger dissipated into simple muscle fatigue, he realized that his license to pulverize parishioners had expired a few centuries ago. If his affluent and influential congregation knew what he was doing, he'd find himself preaching to headhunters in Borneo before he could say 'pass the basket'. He tried to catch his breath as he described the eternal suffering that would be Margo's reward if she told anyone about the incident. She ran home crying and kept her mouth shut.

Margo began to understand her childhood revelation when she took a class in comparative religion. She discovered that cannibalism was the thread that bound the religions of the world together. It tethered the brutal rites of the past to the costumed rituals of the present. Margo could hear muffled screams in the primordial bush beneath the choir hymns that echoed in vast cathedrals. It all began to make sense. Some primitive pagan religions believed that if they ate the flesh of a slain enemy, they gained their victim's strength and skills. As religions evolved and became more complex, their devotees applied the same principal to their deities. When they ritualistically ate their gods, they hoped to gain their spiritual attributes. The fact that it all came down to a theological "You are what you eat" principle disturbed Margo's sense of spiritual transcendence.

She wondered if it could possibly be true. If there wasn't some truth to it, why had cannibalism, real and symbolic, lasted so long? And why was it so prevalent in nature? Countless reptiles and mammals eat their young. Insects like black widow spiders and praying mantises devour their spouses after mating. The more she thought about it, the deeper she sank into a metaphysical mind lagoon. The moist, prickly fire that smoldered in her crack brought her back to reality and she continued looking at the scenery.

The chopper descended quickly as they approached Garien. The rustic woods below gave way to vast expanses of bright green grass. Acres and acres of perfectly manicured lawns separated the colony of huge white colonial mansions from the sea. Margo was still in an anthropological state of mind. She imagined how her exclusive neighborhood would look if she were an anthropologist from another culture. The majestic estates that looked so elegant and imposing at eye level could easily be mistaken for lawn plantations from above. She laughed to herself as she imagined the investment bankers and C.E.O.s as gentleman lawn farmers.

The mental exercise took her mind off her burning ass, so she analyzed them as if they were members of a tribal group. She observed that their kinship system was definitely patrilineal until a form of matriarchy took over when the stressed-out patriarch died young of a coronary. She observed that the inhabitants of the sea-side village practiced a bizarre form of monogamy—serial monogamy to be precise. The men married one woman at a time, but usually kept a younger female on the side in another part of the village.

When it was time to discard the old wife and marry the new one, they went to a tribal elder. The grand patriarch wore a long black costume and struck his table with a small wooden ceremonial hammer. Then the elder ritualistically punished the man by giving some of his prize possessions and sometimes even his children to the discarded wife. The man was then free to marry the new woman. Margo remembered how her father had dumped her mother after 28 years of marriage. Imaginary field work was no longer amusing. She stretched and looked out the window.

The sleek black helicopter hovered above the sprawling Woodbury compound, then gently descended in the middle of their football field size front lawn. The pilot carried Margo's bags up to her room. Her father was waiting impatiently for her to arrive.

The only remaining Woodbury patriarch greeted his daughter with a look of cross affection. Margo read his chaotic thoughts. A jumble of emotions anxiously raced through his cluttered mind. He was not a man who waited well. He stood motionless and annoyed in the center of his enormous entry hall. It reminded her of his stately statue in the lobby of the

Woodbury Building in mid-town Manhattan. In the flesh, he appeared stiffer and somewhat colder than his bronze likeness.

Margo approached her father and delivered the ceremonial Woodbury air-kiss. They both compensated for the lack of physical contact by adding a smoochy sound effect.

She ended the exchange by crooning, "Hi, daddy—luv ya daddy."

Her father glanced at his watch, "I had hoped that you would be dressed for your uncle's funeral when you arrived. Anticipate. You must learn to anticipate, Margo. Run upstairs and get ready. The funeral starts in 30 minutes."

His deep boardroom voice echoed in the emptiness. The huge hall was larger and certainly grander than most single family homes. He was glad to see his only child, but his brother's death commanded his full attention. Margo nodded knowingly and waddled up the stairs like a duck as she picked at the seat of her pants.

When she opened the door to her bedroom, she could see that nothing had changed, except for the bed linen that the upstairs maid changed every Tuesday, whether it needed it or not. Ribbons, trophies and certificates of achievement crowded the walls and shelves of the elegant and spacious room. Margo kicked off her shoes, stripped off her faded Levi's and wiggled out of her uncomfortable underpants. When she examined her practical, pink panties closely, she noticed that the crotch was twisted like a dirty dish rag. Deep creases in the dense cotton cloth were damp with brown, buttery butt juice. A musky ammonia odor wafted from the foreboding folds of the putrid panties. When the air penetrated the inflamed tissue inside the septic crevice of her bare, burning butt, she cried out in anguish and ran in place. Then a morbid sense of urgent curiosity overpowered the painful itch. In a desperate bid for the awful truth, she trotted grotesquely to the full-length mirror in her cavernous, lavender bathroom. With the grace of a hobbled ballerina, she bent at the waist and backed up awkwardly. Margo tucked her head between her legs and scrutinized the lurid reflection of her upside-down, posterior presentation. She cautiously spread her chaffed cheeks and gasped at the disgusting display. It became painfully clear that a careless wipe was the cause of her irritating condition.

Brittle, brown flecks of feces caked her throbbing, bright magenta sphincter. The tender flesh all around her crusty crack was raw and red. Just looking at the irksome irritation made her rare rump burn even more. Margo had seen enough. She crumpled a wad of toilet paper and took an agonizing swipe at the reeking residue. The pillowy soft toilet tissue felt like coarse sandpaper. She winced and grabbed a container of baby powder from the medicine cabinet. Her hands trembled as she dusted her inflamed fanny. It didn't help. Margo shuddered in pain and revulsion. In a brave attempt to regain her dignity, she stood up straight and struck a regal pose. Then she stumbled—bowlegged—to her closet.

It looked more like a department store warehouse than a closet. The clothes she'd taken to college didn't even dent her formidable wardrobe. She wove through row after row of designer outfits until a conservative black dress caught her eye. Margo slipped into it quickly and stepped into a fresh pair of panties. Then she pulled out "The Drawer of Doom," a special drawer in her armoire where she kept all her funeral accessories. She reached inside and pulled out her funeral ensemble: black patent leather pumps with black satin bows, black pillbox hat, black veil, black eel skin purse, black onyx broach and a stack of white linen hankies—just in case.

Then Margo surveyed her outfit, from every conceivable angle, in the maze of mirrors that surrounded her dressing room. It was perfect—a marvelously mournful medley of black on black. Margo wasn't beautiful, but she was a handsome young woman. She still had a few pounds of baby-fat that

softened the angular contours of her strong, athletic body. The combination of her dark brown hair and black tailored dress complemented her pale smooth complexion and cold gray-blue eyes. There was just a touch of horsiness in her well-defined features. Perhaps a few drops of blue blood had hitched a ride across the Atlantic in the seventeenth century. Margo admired her funeral fashion statement in the mirror, then ran downstairs to join her bereaved father.

The chauffeur was warming up the black Rolls reserved for solemn occasions. Charles Woodbury made some last minute arrangements on the phone in his study. Margo had just enough time, before the funeral, to take a quick peek at her bunnies. She grabbed a carrot from the kitchen counter as she ran to the rabbit hutch behind the stables. She knelt down and looked inside. Three newborn bunnies slept peacefully in their cozy, hay lined nest. Their mother lay cuddled next to them. It was Buffy, a pure white Angora doe that Margo had raised when she was still in high school.

She opened the door to the hutch and petted Buffy's thick soft fur. Margo remembered stroking her for hours while her parents argued upstairs in the big house. Buffy always made Margo feel warm and safe. Now Buffy had a little family of her own.

The baby bunnies looked naked and helpless as they huddled together for warmth and comfort. Buffy gently licked her babies. The smallest of the litter clumsily rolled over on its back. Buffy slowly nuzzled her baby's soft round belly as it quivered in delight.

Then, without warning, The attentive mother rabbit sank her broad chiseled teeth into her baby's soft, bulging belly. Its thin translucent skin ripped open easily. The bare, blind baby desperately tried to wiggle away. Buffy viciously sank her teeth deeper into her squirming, squealing spawn. Margo watched helplessly, paralyzed with horror, as Buffy gnawed deep into her baby's gaping abdomen. The carrot fell from Margo's hand as the baby bunny quivered and died.

Sticky, scarlet patches of fresh blood soiled Buffy's soft, white fur. A tangle of viscera and veins dangled menacingly from her mouth. She looked up at Margo with wild red eyes. Margo tried to look away, but there was a sense of urgency in the rabbit's gaze. Margo sensed that Buffy was trying to tell her something important. She slowly began to comprehend what was in the rabbit's mind. The communication was not in words. The thought patterns were abstract and disorganized, but the intention was clear. Buffy wanted Margo to pick up her dead baby. Confused and upset, Margo complied with Buffy's command. She reached into the hutch and gently scooped up the bloody body of the lifeless little bunny. As she cupped it tenderly in her hands, Margo looked down at Buffy. The baby was some kind of offering—Buffy killed it for her. Margo felt sick as the baby's blood dripped through her fingers. As Buffy rose up on her haunches, a flood of primitive drives and terrifying impulses swept into Margo's mind. Her whole body trembled when Buffy's intentions became clear.

Margo shook her head and cried, "No Buffy, I can't do it!"

The rabbit's thoughts were strong and focused. The absolute horror of Buffy's command made Margo want to run away, but she couldn't break the strange hold that her fluffy pet had on her.

She started to cry and pleaded with the rabbit, "Please don't make me do it, Buffy! Why are you doing this to me?"

Buffy's telepathic command was too strong. Margo couldn't fight it any longer. She raised the baby bunny to her lips and sunk her teeth deep into its tiny body. Then she ripped off a stringy strip of flesh and swallowed it with tears in her eyes. Margo dropped to her knees and screamed in horror. The bony little corpse fell from her hands. Confused and afraid, she winced as the slippery morsel of rubbery meat slid slowly down her gullet. Then a profound sense of calm and well-being swept over her. Suddenly, everything that had just occurred seemed totally natural and normal.

In a heartbeat, Margo possessed animal instincts that she never experienced before. Her metaphysical questions about cannibalism were answered instantly. The mysteries that she had struggled with for so long, intellectually, became clear to her, instinctively. Every cell in her body vibrated with the secret knowledge of nature. She reached into the hutch and gently touched Buffy on the cheek. The eerie rabbit licked the blood from Margo's fingers. There was now an unbreakable bond between them. Margo clearly understood everything that Buffy was thinking.

The rabbit's thought-words were like gentle whispers, "I thought you needed to know. Knowing is being. Now part of us is part of you. Your kind has been blessed with forgetfulness. You are part of nature, but you only live nature's dream. Now nature is awake in you. Experience the world with all your senses."

Margo rose silently and closed the door to the rabbit hutch. Buffy went back to her two remaining babies. A horn honked in the distance. She grabbed her purse and ran to the front of the estate. A slight hop was evident in her graceful gait. Her father motioned to her impatiently as the driver held the back door of the Rolls open. She slid across the long, tan leather seat next to her father.

He frowned and said, "Did you bite your lip? There's blood in the corner of your mouth."

Margo took a tissue from her purse and dabbed the glistening scarlet smudge. She crumpled the tissue and tossed it out the window. It fell to the ground like a delicate red and white paper carnation. The broad black tires of the Rolls tore it to bits as it sped down the long cobblestone driveway. Massive wrought iron gates flung open automatically as they rolled onto the Old Fort Road and rushed towards the church cemetery.

It was a lovely morning for a funeral. The sky was clear and a warm breeze blew in from the sea. The azaleas were in bloom. A French Impressionist could not have arranged them more artfully. A pastel pallet of lavender, pink and fusha spattered the sprawling meadows. Margo stared out the window. Everything looked the same, but somehow she felt different. As they sped past the lush landscape, she longed to run naked through the tall green grass. The azaleas smelled more intense than she ever remembered.

Margo's butt still burned furiously. But this time she had an uncontrollable urge to lick the inflamed area. She covered her mouth to stifle a chuckle. Her father glared at her with a shocked, pissed-off expression. Margo turned her head so he couldn't see her. They rode to the cemetery in silence.

The Woodburys arrived at the cemetery late. When they pulled into the church parking lot, the funeral cortege had already arrived. It looked as if all the limos in New England were there. An army of uniformed drivers talked and smoked in cloistered groups. Margo and her father walked briskly towards the Woodbury mausoleum that dominated the center of the old cemetery.

It was obvious that the stygian structure was architecturally significant. Even in death, the Woodburys projected an image of wealth and power. Margo's grandfather, William Woodbury, had commissioned Frank Lloyd Wright to design the family's final resting place. The imposing edifice was a classic example of the architect's Mayan period. From a distance it appeared to be a cross between a mesoamerican monument and an austere artillery bunker. Close-up, it embodied the very essence of death. It was cold, dark, empty and eternal.

As a child, Margo had nightmares about being swallowed by its inky emptiness. She grew older, but the menacing mausoleum always remained the same. It had all the time in

the world, but she did not. She knew that eventually she'd become a part of its crumbling collection of Woodburys—carefully filed away for eternity in their cramped little niches. She thought about the mausoleum often. Sometimes she could hear it call to her inside her head. Wherever she was, whatever she was doing, she knew that the sinister sepulcher was waiting patiently in the old churchyard.

Today, it was Uncle Hilton's turn. Who would be next? Margo and her father walked up the aisle arm in arm. Charles Woodbury looked like the father of the bride at a black wedding. Hundreds of moneyed mourners fidgeted and whispered among themselves. At first glance, it appeared that the Reverend Thomas J. Aldridge had performed a minor miracle by parting a sea of folding metal chairs. He stood at the end of the narrow aisle —his arms in the air. A rippling wave of turning heads followed Margo and her father as they marched toward the mausoleum. Margo could hear the crowd chattering in her head. Some were admiring her outfit, some were admiring her tits—some just wondered why they were so late.

Hilton Woodbury had been an important man. He was a captain of industry and an advisor to three presidents. Two of them were in attendance. Every C.E.O. east of the Rockies was there. The thought that he had kept them all waiting made Charles Woodbury wish that he could change places with his brother.

The burning itch in Margo's crack was unbearable. As they neared the mausoleum, her long, confident strides degenerated into a waddling swagger. She wanted to scratch her ass so bad she could scream, but Margo fought the urge—Uncle Hilton and the Reverend were waiting.

As Margo and her father approached the imposing, bronze casket, the Reverend seemed somewhat perturbed. Uncle Hilton didn't seem to mind the wait. He looked great for a man in his condition. The cosmetician had done an outstanding job. He appeared tan and serene—two things he'd never been in life. He looked remarkably sharp and powerful for a cadaver. Despite the old adage, he was taking some of his personal power symbols with him. He would be sailing down the River Styx wearing his black double breasted power suit by Daniel Schagen, gold power watch by Rolex, white 100% cotton power shirt by Van Laack and pure silk power tie by Brioni. He looked better dead than most men look alive.

An impressive array of floral arrangements surrounded the casket. The heavy iron doors of the mausoleum were wide open, but it was still dark inside. The hideous place ate sunlight and excreted gloom. The smell of "old money," alive and dead, permeated the stale air. Reverend Aldridge began his eulogy with a litany of Uncle Hilton's accomplishments. He droned on and on in a mournful monotone. As the Reverend mixed and matched the usual selection of holy scriptures with snippets of pop philosophy, Margo began to fade. Her lack of sleep had finally caught up with her and she felt light headed. She skipped breakfast that morning and dinner the night before. Her knees were rubbery and she began to wobble. The more she tried to maintain a vertical and pious posture, the more she swayed.

There was no place to sit down. In desperation, she slowly inched her way toward the wall. At least she could lean with a certain amount of comfort. After a few minutes she reached her destination. The cool damp concrete blocks were a welcome relief. Frank Lloyd Wright had personally designed their marginally Mayan motif. She rested her back against the blocks and sighed. The stark geometry of their pattern pressed deep into her back, but she didn't mind. After a few moments, an added benefit to her new location became clear. The towering floral displays that cluttered the stately crypt hid Margo from view. She seized the moment and scratched her ass. It felt so good that she reached up the back of her dress and rooted around her prickly crack like a butt-badger.

As Reverend Aldridge's rambling requiem entered its second hour, Margo's thoughts began to wander. She surveyed the names chiseled in the marble fascia that sealed her dead relative's cramped cubicles. In an attempt to stay awake, she studied the dates below the names and calculated their age when they died. Then she imagined her own name engraved in crisp Roman serif type on one of the four unoccupied rectangular voids. She wondered which claustrophobic cubbyhole would be her home for all eternity. The hungry holes seemed to draw her into their greedy emptiness.

She scrutinized them one by one. Suddenly, she was sure she found the right one. A damp chill crept into her bones as she stared at the vacant vault to the left of her cousin Chad. Margo remembered him as a quirky kid with a mean streak a mile wide. He was a mathematical genius and his family let him get away with murder.

He died three years earlier, under strange circumstances. Chad was only 23 years old when he shuffled off his mortal coil. Apparently he hung himself. He was home for the holidays from M.I.T., where he was doing research in quantum physics. The family told everyone his death was suicide, but he didn't leave a note. A few days after the funeral his younger sister Kathleen told Margo all the gory details.

When his mother returned home from jogging, she found him dangling at the end of a long silk scarf that belonged to his sister. It was tied to a large eye-hook secured to the ceiling above his bed. The upper part of his body was pale and sallow and his lower extremities were purple and bloated. His eyes bulged half out of their sockets. His tongue was blue and swollen. Strange black rubber underpants draped around his ankles.

The room smelled like a roadside restroom from the sudden release of his body's waste and gases. Perverse pornography depicting bondage and sadistic sex blanketed his bed. Chad's body was limp and lifeless—except for a full erection. The bulging boner pointed accusingly at everyone who entered the room. It swayed like a demented dowsing rod as his body slowly twisted back and forth.

The police said that they'd seen similar situations before. According to them, Chad indulged in a bizarre masochistic masturbation ritual that had simply gone too far. They said it was more common than most people imagined. Margo had always known that Chad was a horny little shit, but she never imagined that he was that far gone.

Once during a family gathering, when Margo was thirteen, Chad cornered her in the boat house and groped her when no one was around. He laughed and said he was just checking to see if she was still a virgin. Margo kneed him in the nuts and ran to the house. When she told her father about what Chad had done Margo's father got mad at her and called her a little slut.

The thought of spending eternity next to Chad didn't appeal to Margo much. She wondered if she could specify the location of her eventual internment. There was a vacancy next to Aunt Erica. She was 93 years old when she died in a fire—at least that was the official cause of death. It was certainly the one that the Woodbury family endorsed. Aunt Erica had been a famous concert pianist and contemporary classical composer. After her aunt's death, Margo read an article in a sleazy tabloid that gave her pause for thought. The publisher managed to get his hands on a photograph taken by the county coroner. It showed every detail of Aunt Erica's ghastly remains and burned-out bathroom. The dubious newspaper featured the revolting color picture on the cover.

The walls and ceiling were black with soot. Intense heat had burned a huge hole through the floor. The kitchen was clearly visible below. Her aluminum walker surrounded the opening like a guard rail around an open manhole. It was painfully obvious that Aunt Erica had exploded. Her dismembered feet straddled the smoking hole—still snug in their fuzzy, blue slippers. Everything above the ankles was gone. Blackened bone protruded from the mangled mass of blistered meat. The picture clearly showed delicate wisps of oily smoke billowing from the grizzly stumps. A few charred strips of saggy skin and some matted hunks of coarse gray hair were all that remained of Aunt Erica. Her seared remnants dangled from scorched joists and melted plumbing in the incinerated bathroom. Bold headline type above the lurid photo read: "COMPOSER DIES OF SPONTANEOUS COMBUSTION."

Margo wondered if there was something incendiary about beets. Aunt Erica always bragged that she drank three large glasses of beet juice every day. Once when Margo was nine, her aunt forced her to drink a warm glass of beet juice. She caught Margo sneaking a dish of vanilla ice cream before dinner. As punishment, Aunt Erica went to the pantry and opened a can of thick magenta beet-sludge. When she poured it into a tall plastic glass, the pungent metallic odor made Margo gag—one sip of the noxious red slime and she threw up instantly. The beet juice and ice cream mixed together as they both came up. Margo could still see the swirling pink and white puddle of puke on her aunt's yellow speckled linoleum floor. Maybe a final resting place directly under Aunt Erica wasn't such a good idea. Margo cringed at the thought of what might ooze through the cracks, over the centuries, from all those beet saturated bits and pieces.

There was a space available to the right of Courtney Woodbury, Margo's stepmother. She died last November, only two years after marrying Charles Woodbury. He dumped Margo's mother for Courtney after 28 years of marriage. When Margo's parents married, the perky temptress hadn't even been born. Charles met Courtney when the Woodbury Foundation bestowed a large grant on her modern dance troop. He presented the endowment check at the gala opening of their first performance. They talked and flirted at the cast party after the show. A cash register bell chimed in Courtney's head and a rocket went off in Charles' pocket.

Courtney was blond and beautiful. Her body was agile and well-rounded—her brain was neither. She had a perfect figure, but she constantly searched for ways to make it better. When she got her hands on the vast Woodbury resources, she entered a narcissistic nirvana. She spent the first six months of marriage building her wardrobe and the next couple of months getting her hair just right. Looking good was Courtney's job, her religion, her reason for being.

After a while, she was no longer content with beauty parlors and exclusive spas. She really hit her stride when she discovered the wondrous world of cosmetic surgery. Practically overnight, Courtney was on a first name basis with every knife jockey on the East Coast. She stepped up for breast implants, a tummy tuck, liposuction—the works.

As soon as one surgical procedure had healed, she was ready for another. Even her belly button was up for grabs. Through the miracle of modern medicine she had it changed from an outy to an iny. Courtney looked great, but Margo was miserable. Her real mother was a basket case after the divorce and her father was constantly frustrated and pissed off. Charles hadn't gotten much action since he married Courtney. His high-performance princess was either in the shop or too sore to touch from all her operations.

Eventually Charles put his foot down. He told Courtney that she couldn't have any more plastic surgery. She was crushed. For weeks, she whined and cried and wouldn't come out of her room. Charles eventually weakened and agreed to one last operation. Courtney was ecstatic. She knew exactly what she wanted to have done—her nose *again.* After three nose jobs, she still wasn't satisfied.

A few months earlier, she had her lips pumped up with collagen. Now they were plump and pouty, but Courtney felt that they clashed with what remained of her nose. When she went in for one last nose job everything went smoothly—until it was time to remove the bandages. Courtney had seen her doctor do it so often that she decided to remove the dressing herself. She left the bandage on a few extra days to make sure all the swelling and bruises were gone.

Courtney wanted to surprise everyone with her new nose. Charles, Margo and the entire household staff assembled for the unveiling. When she removed the final white gauze rectangle, everyone gasped. All that remained of her nose was a black, shriveled nub. Courtney ran to the mirror above the mantle and fainted when she saw her revolting reflection. Charles rushed her to the emergency room, but the doctors could do nothing. Her nose became gangrenous under the bandages. When the surgeon cut away all the dead festering flesh, there was no nose left. All that remained was an up-side-down heart-shaped hole in the center of her face. Courtney looked like the Phantom of the Opera's daughter.

The hideous hole was raw and infected. Her gristly white septum projected from the tainted tissue that rotted inside her head. Thick green, blood-streaked snot oozed endlessly from the ominous orifice. Whenever she tried to speak or eat, the reeking runoff poured into her mouth and made her gag. The doctors sent her home with a full time nurse, but Courtney's condition deteriorated rapidly.

Margo and her father removed every mirror in the house so Courtney couldn't see what she had become. Charles reassured her that as soon as the infection cleared up, he would buy her the best prosthetic nose that money could buy. But Courtney was inconsolable. She just shuffled from room to room. A plastic cup strapped under her chin caught the gangrenous puss that dripped incessantly. Sometimes she'd sit for hours and page through old photo albums. She desperately grieved for her perky little nose. Day by day, her will to live weakened. Finally, the infection in her nose spread to her brain and within two days she was dead.

Margo remembered Courtney's funeral. It was cold and rainy. Only a handful of people came to see her off. Most of them were Courtney's relatives. Only one of her doctor friends showed up. He sat by himself with a sheepish expression on his face—like Victor Frankenstein after the villagers took away his monster. Margo's father didn't say much, he didn't even cry. Mercifully, it was a closed casket affair. Courtney would have wanted it that way. Unlike this morning, Reverend Aldridge concluded the service in 20 minutes. He seemed more like a servant tidying up his master's mess than a shepherd of souls. They neatly filed Courtney away and that was the end of that.

Margo was getting bored with the idea of selecting her final resting place. When it came right down to it, they all sucked. Funerals sucked. Being dead sucked. Being a dead Woodbury double sucked.

"Woodburys don't die like normal people," she thought. "We always die of something weird or goofy. We never die of something simple like a heart attack or a car accident. God only knows what actually caused Uncle Hilton's death."

Margo's father told her that he died in his sleep, but that could mean just about anything. Margo figured that in a few days she'd get the real story. Whatever he died of, she was certain of one thing—It was something embarrassing.

Uncle Hilton's cubicle had a small brown curtain covering the opening. Did it conceal some dark secret that only dead Woodburys and Frank Lloyd Wright were permitted to know? Margo's mind began drifting. Her eyelids were getting so heavy that she finally gave in and closed them for a moment. It felt too good.

Reverend Aldridge's voice droned on in a slow measured monotone. Since no one could see her, Margo sat down and tried to get her strength back. She eased down to the floor and rested her head on one of the massive floral wreaths that surrounded her. Every cell in her body sighed with relief. The Reverend's voice faded in and out. Her muscles relaxed and her breathing slowed. A warm blanket of darkness covered her as she plunged into a deep dreamless sleep.

Margo sat up with an awkward spasm. Her eyes sprung open and stared into the black void that surrounded her. The air was thick with the sweet rot of flesh and flowers. She pulled her numb right hand from under her sweaty torso. A prickly swarm of sensation buzzed in her paralyzed fingers. Panic jolted her muddled senses. Margo was alone in the Woodbury mausoleum. Her heart raced. A hot surge of adrenaline flooded every groggy fiber of her trembling body. Margo was awake. She sprang to her feet and clawed the oppressive darkness. Something brushed her cheek. She jumped straight up like a startled rabbit and crashed on top of a huge, unseen funeral wreath. Panting and shaking, she rolled off and collapsed in a heap on the cold, damp marble floor.

Her childhood nightmare had come true. The ravenous mausoleum had swallowed her alive. She was a frightened little girl, small and alone, in the cold, black belly of death. The gluttonous sepulcher had an insatiable appetite for Woodburys. It had been slowly digesting her relatives for over six decades. But it still wasn't satisfied. They'd fallen into its dark, gaping mouth, one by one. Now it was Margo's turn.

A hot stream of urine gushed under her dress. Margo whimpered to the rhythm of her frantic breathing. She groped in the darkness, desperately searching for a way out. She left a

wet trail of pee behind her as she slithered across the floor like a blind slug. "Maybe the Reverend left the doors unlocked," she thought. Her trembling fingertips touched something smooth and cool. She fingered a series of deep intricate grooves and realized that they were letters—engraved on a marble slab. It was the wall. She inched her way around the perimeter until she found the massive doors. They felt cold and rough. A brisk draft rushed through the crack between the solid, rusty metal monoliths. She flung herself against them and pushed with all her strength—they didn't budge. Her small, bare fists barely made a thud as she pounded wildly on the thick, icy, iron doors. A faint echo of hopelessness reverberated deep in the hollow center of her being. When it reached the surface of her consciousness, it exploded in a silent shock wave of total despair. She clawed at the unyielding iron and tried to scream. Her rib cage rattled as her lungs forced the air up and out of her body, but there was no sound. It was if she had screamed in a vacuum. The absorbent emptiness of the dense, black void sucked the scream from her throat before it could reach her ears.

Margo dropped to the floor and curled up in a quivering ball. Her spirit felt naked in the leering darkness, her flesh vulnerable to unseen violations. She pulled her flailing extremities close to her chest. They jerked in a spastic release of fear and panic. Then her body stiffened. Vertebrae and joints creaked and popped as her muscles tensed in one violent spasm. Margo lay rigid and motionless. A muffled whisper wormed its way through the silence. At first it was too faint to understand. Then the sinister sound grew louder. As it squirmed inside her head, she realized that it wasn't a single voice. Dozens of voices surrounded her. The hideous chorus crooned her name—"Margo"—over and over. She recognized some of the disembodied voices: Aunt Erica, Cousin Chad, Courtney and Uncle Hilton.

The eerie voices seemed to emanate from the walls of the

mausoleum. Margo covered her ears, but the sound reverberated inside her head. The chorus continued, "M a r—go." The ghastly sound grew louder and rose in pitch. It separated the syllables of her name and stretched it out. The voices echoed with a shaky sing-song tremolo.

"Something about all this is goofy," Margo mumbled to herself.

The voices were *too* spooky. They were so spooky that they were no longer frightening. The melodramatic caterwauling sounded like a hammed up voice-over from an Abbott and Costello ghost movie. Margo fully expected to hear Lou yell, "Hey, Abbott!" Margo's fear quickly turned to anger. She was really pissed. With a renewed sense of purpose, she rose to her feet. The chorus called her name again, "*M a r—g o.*"

With her hands on her hips, she shouted back, "Yea, that's my name, worm meat—don't wear it out! What the fuck do you want?"

There was a moment of silence.

Then only Chad's voice replied, "We want you, Margo. We've been waiting for you. Now you're one of us."

Margo was furious, "I'm not one of you, jerk-off. You're dead and I'm alive."

The decomposing deviate yelled back, "You won't be alive much longer! How long do you think you'll last without food or water?"

Margo thought for a minute. She *was* hungry and thirsty, but she wasn't about to give Chad any satisfaction.

She yelled back, "I can go a long time without food or water, dickmeister, but I won't have to. As soon as Daddy notices I'm gone, he'll come back for me."

From across the crypt Courtney chimed in, "Margo could live for weeks off that fat ass of hers."

Margo called back, "Keep your nose-hole out of this—you snotty bitch."

From above and to her left, she could hear her Aunt Erica's shaky voice, "I hope you drank your beet juice this morning, Honey. It's going to be a long time before you get out of here."

Then all her rotting relatives started chattering at once. They taunted and threatened her, but Margo just ignored them. Her instincts for survival were strong. The more they tried to frighten her, the more determined she became to live. If she could just hold on long enough, she knew that help would come.

"What I need now is a little light," she thought.

She searched for a light switch for over an hour—no luck. Apparently the practical Mr. Wright felt that the dead had no need for illumination.

In total darkness, Margo fumbled her way back to where she'd fallen asleep. She found her purse, removed a book of matches and eagerly struck one. The tiny flickering flame penetrated the darkness. It revealed a large decorative candelabra in the corner. Cupping the match, she walked toward it and lit several large candles. The soft, warm light instantly gave form and dimension to her macabre environment.

The chorus chanted, "All the better to see you *die* with, my dear."

Margo paid no attention as she relished the return of her sense of sight.

She sat down and analyzed the situation. It didn't look much better, but at least it was brighter. Her dead relatives were annoying, but they didn't pose any tangible threat. An adequate supply of air seemed to be flowing through the small spaces around the outer perimeter of the door. Food and water were the critical factors.

Margo looked around. The countless floral arrangements she'd noticed that morning were sill there. There was also some equipment that the funeral attendants had left behind. She walked over to the flowers and inspected them more closely. There were small plastic vials of water at the bottom of the stems. Some of the larger floral arrangements rested in huge ceramic vases—half full of the precious liquid. She picked one up, removed the flowers and sipped the room temperature water. It was bitter and a little slimy, but it was wet. Water would not be an immediate problem. What she found would last for weeks. She reasoned that before the water ran out, her father would notice that she was missing and return to the mausoleum.

Food was the real problem. She was already famished. It had been over 24 hours since she'd eaten anything. Her empty stomach growled and churned. Having the piss scared out of her really gave Margo an appetite. She rooted around in her purse for something to eat. All she could find was a lint covered after-dinner-mint—lurking at the bottom of the bag. She popped it into her mouth and sucked on it as she pondered her predicament.

Chad rudely interrupted her train of thought, "Well aren't we cozy? Soft candle light, pretty flowers, a little something to drink, all you need now is food, and a little dinner music. Remember those summer cookouts at Aunt April's house on the lake? As I recall, you were partial to barbecued chicken. How'd you like to bite into a tender breast right now. What about that crispy blackened skin—covered with your daddy's secret, Texas-style sauce? Can't you just taste that juicy white meat now?"

Margo crossed her arms over her stomach.

An empty ache gnawed inside her, as Chad continued. "How about some of Aunt April's homemade potato salad and Boston baked beans?"

Chad touched a nerve.

Margo twisted and turned as he tortured her more, "Or maybe I could interest you in a big piece of hot apple pie, right out of the oven. Hey Margo, how about a scoop of French vanilla ice cream on that pie?"

Margo couldn't take it any more. Something snapped in her head. Her hunger had reached critical mass. Her appetite exploded in a frenzy for food. She jumped up and threw a vase at Chad's niche in the wall. It was a direct hit. Chad laughed luridly. The rest of the relatives joined in. The sound was deafening.

Margo shook her head and cried, "STOP IT!"

Saliva frothed around her snarling mouth as she howled at her jeering relations, "Dinner is served, you dead dick-heads! You're on the menu tonight! I'll eat your rotting hearts and shit your black souls!"

With that, Margo ran to the lift that the funeral attendants had used to hoist Uncle Hilton's casket into place. She rolled it over to Chad's niche and raised it until it was level with the opening. Then she grabbed a heavy hammer the workers had left on the roller-lined floor of the lift. Margo smashed through the shiny, gray Italian marble, slid Chad's coffin onto the rollers and lowered it to the floor. The voices had died down to a chorus of soft murmurs and hushed whispers. With several sure hammer blows, Margo cracked open Chad's coffin the way an impatient diner cracks a lobster shell—greedy for the sweet meat inside.

She pulled at Chad's clothes. His shirt and tie and coat came off in one easy tug. They were open in the back to make the mortician's job easier. In an instant his pants were off. He lay there dead and naked, surrounded by the white pleated satin that lined his coffin. His skin was pale and gray. Except for his face, which had a thick layer of greasy makeup that crinkled on his festering features.

The mortician had sewn Chad's unruly hard-on to his abdomen—a dignified precaution that kept it from popping up at the funeral. It was shriveled like a dry carrot. Margo

reached down and ripped the petrified penis out at the roots. She gazed into the sunken holes where Chad's eyes once shined.

Margo smiled and said, "This looks like a tasty appetizer. You won't be needing it any more, will you Chad?"

She crunched down on the puckered pecker and tore off the withered tip.

Chad's disembodied voice moaned in mock ecstasy, "Oh Margo, you know what I like."

She gnawed another chewy chunk and spit out the dried veins and rubbery connective tissue. Then she tossed the leathery remnants over her shoulder and circled the coffin in search of an entree.

A long, crudely stitched incision extended from the center of Chad's clavicle to the top of his pubic bone. Margo used a sharp shard from the broken vase to pop the thick sutures. Then she pried open his rib cage. Foul vapors made her eyes tear. The stench of rotting flesh, organic gases and formaldehyde filled the crypt.

The gaping cavity was a jumbled mess of vital organs and unrecognizable muck. The medical examiner had cut him open, measured and weighed his organs, then simply tossed them back and stitched him up. She plunged her hand into the slimy slop and fished around until she felt something large and spongy—Chad's heart. It dripped with slippery suet and sinewy sludge.

Chad's voice echoed in the air above his corpse, "Will you be my valentine, Margo?"

She squeezed the pickled pump in her fist. It squished between her fingers. Clear runny juice squirted everywhere.

Chad whined snidely, "Oh Margo, you're breaking my heart."

She sank her teeth into the mangled muscle and tore off a mealy chunk. It was foul and fibrous. As she chomped away in disgust, the rancid flesh burned her tender mouth.

Chad crooned, "Bon appétit."

Margo replied, "I've heard about enough out of you," and threw what was left of Chad's heart at the wall.

It impacted with a squishy splat, plopped on the floor, quivered for a moment, then slumped silently in a puddle of its own vile juice.

Margo examined Chad's head. She gently ran her fingers across his forehead.

Chad yelled, "Leave my head alone!" He sounded upset.

Margo replied, "Oh, you don't like that—do you, Chad? What's the matter? Afraid I might do—*this*?"

She firmly grasped either side of his grotesque head—just above the temples—and pulled hard. The top of Chad's head popped off like a hard, bony cap—scalp and all. Margo was relieved to see that the medical examiner had the courtesy to put Chad's brain back where it belonged. His "genius" cortex had turned into a gray, gooshy glob. She reached into his cranial cavity and scooped up the morbid mass of mush.

Chad screamed, "NO!"

Margo slurped the slimy brain-pudding like oysters on the half shell.

As Chad's brain filled Margo's empty stomach, it filled her head with numbers. Esoteric theorems spun in a churning vortex of subtle particles and abstract waves. Space and time twisted in strange dualities as Margo's mind absorbed Chad's mastery of quantum mechanics. Margo felt dizzy from the sudden influx of information. Luckily, It was only Chad's genius that merged into her being, not his perversions.

Margo felt a sudden pressure deep in her abdomen. She squatted, and groaned. A long, melodic, foul smelling fart echoed in the cavernous vault. The reeking condensation of Chad's corrupted essence dissipated in an invisible cloud of gaseous atoms. In a nanosecond, Margo's caustic cousin had vanished—gone forever in one flatulent singularity.

Margo pushed Chad's mangled coffin out of the way and rolled the lift over to Courtney's cubicle. She couldn't wait to exhume Daddy's putrefying princess. When Margo cracked open Courtney's coffin, she laughed so hard she began to hiccup. Courtney looked ridiculous. In the short time she'd been interred, she had not decomposed gracefully.

Courtney's voice shrieked above Margo's laughter, "Close my coffin, you bitch. I don't want anyone to see me like this!"

Margo ripped off Courtney's white silk negligee and howled even harder. Courtney was quite a sight to see. Moisture had penetrated her rot upholstered coffin. Her hair looked like a frizzy fright-wig. A dark brown corona of dusty roots circled her forehead where her bleached blond hair had grown out. Her fingernails had continued growing from her withered fingertips. The curly yellow nails had bright red nail polish tips. They looked like monster claws from a low budget science fiction movie. The funniest thing of all was the remarkable condition of Courtney's tits. They were just as perky as ever. The rest of Courtney's body was sunken and wrinkled, but her silicone breast implants were smooth, firm and high—pointing strait to heaven.

Once, Courtney's lips were full and pouty. Now, they stretched tight across her dry toothy grin. A long black worm crawled out of her gaping nose-hole. Margo watched with fascination as the worm meandered around Courtney's hideous face. It wiggled and writhed from cheek to chin and from ear to ear. The inquisitive invertebrate eagerly explored the decomposing gore-goddess' crumbling countenance. Eventually, the worm got tired and curled up for a nap above Courtney's upper lip.

That was the final touch. Margo roared. Now Courtney looked like a cadaverous Salvador Dali—*in drag*. Tears poured down Margo's cheeks as she laughed hysterically. She held on to Courtney's casket for support, but collapsed, howling, on

the cold, damp floor. She rocked back and forth and tried to catch her breath.

Margo's laughter was infectious. A few of the spirit voices began to chuckle, then a few more. In a matter of moments, all the dead Woodburys were wailing hysterically.

All except Courtney, "I fail to see the humor here!"

Her prissy protest only intensified the laughter. The sound was deafening.

Suddenly, a loud pounding echoed in the mausoleum. All at once the laughter stopped.

A voice on the other side of the huge iron doors demanded, "WHO'S IN THERE?"

The voice was authoritative—accustomed to projecting at considerable volume.

Margo recognized it immediately and answered, "It's me Reverend Aldridge—Margo Woodbury."

"What on earth are you doing in there at this hour?" The Reverend sounded confused.

"I've been locked in here since Uncle Hilton's funeral. Let me out!"

Margo heard the rattle of keys, then the sharp metallic snap of the huge dead bolt. The massive doors slowly swung open. Rusty hinges screeched in protest. A gust of cool night air rushed in and replaced the stale, thick atmosphere inside the tomb. Reverend Aldridge poked his flashlight through the opening and cautiously entered the crypt.

He stood there in his baggy cotton nightshirt and whispered, "Margo—where are you?"

She whispered back, "I'm over here."

The Reverend aimed his flashlight in the direction of Margo's voice. The bright beam illuminated the dim, candlelit carnage in the corner. He gasped and reeled backwards from the utter depravity that confronted him.

Margo crouched next to Courtney's coffin like a wild

animal. Clotted clumps of decomposing carnage clung to her mouth and caked her tattered black dress.

Reverend Aldridge shouted, "What in heaven's name is going on in here?"

Margo shielded her eyes from his flashlight's glare and snapped back, "Just let me out of here!"

The Reverend shivered with disgust.

In a ghoulish attempt to tidy-up, Margo began stuffing yard-long loops of Courtney's ropey viscera back in the cadaver's empty abdominal cavity.

As Margo wrestled with the last few feet, she sheepishly muttered an explanation, "I had to survive, I could have starved to death in here."

The Reverend looked confused and replied, "But your uncle's funeral was just this morning! This is an abomination!"

He walked toward Margo, stopped suddenly and groaned, "Ugh—what the hell?"

His flashlight illuminated his bare feet. He jumped back and screamed when he realized that he stepped on the rancid remains of Chad's mangled heart. Putrid pulp from the mushy muscle oozed between his toes. Margo laughed as he danced around the crypt, trying to shake the flesh off his chubby bare foot. Margo's laughter made the Reverend furious.

He shook his flashlight at her and launched into a tirade, "Spawn of Satan, with your blasphemous questions and smart talk! And now you eat the blessed dead!"

The Reverend's thoughts screamed louder than his words. Horrible images burned in his brain. Margo saw a mental image of herself stretched out naked on a wooden rack. The Reverend jabbed hot pokers into her soft, pale flesh as he commanded her to recant. Then she saw herself burning at the stake. Margo backed up as Reverend Aldridge's thoughts became more hideous and threatening. He lunged at Margo and grabbed her by the throat.

Tightening his grip, he screamed, "DEVIL BITCH!"

There was murder in his mind. When Margo shifted her weight to avoid his attack, the Reverend lost his balance and slid on a slippery glob of brain-pudding. With his arms flailing wildly, he stumbled forward with considerable momentum. His feet slipped out from under him and he was airborne. He took a flying nose dive right on top of Courtney's corpse. The full weight of his stout body split the bloated cadaver open like a rotten pumpkin. A geyser of gore gushed from the sides of her ornate casket. The Reverend hit his head inside the lead-lined coffin—he was down for the count.

Margo heard sirens approaching from The Old Fort Road. The odd, flickering light inside the eerie edifice alerted the suspicious local police. She quickly grabbed her purse and ran outside. The sirens wailed louder as she dove into the bushes just beyond the entrance of the mausoleum. A pack of squad-cars cut across the cemetery. Flashing red light illuminated clouds of grave-dust as they fishtailed through an obstacle course of granite headstones. The dusty black and whites screeched to a stop in front of the mausoleum. With guns drawn, the uniformed officers jumped out of their cars and bounded through the gaping metal doors of the cavernous crypt.

Margo peeked inside just in time to see them surround Reverend Aldridge. He was beginning to regain consciousness. When he started to climb out of the coffin, two of the officers turned and ran in terror. The Reverend looked like a zombie rising from the dead. Most of what remained of Courtney's gelatinous corpse dripped from the reverend as he continued to rise. Her greasy makeup covered his grimacing face. He was the last thing anybody wanted to see in a cemetery—in the middle of the night.

A news crew from the local TV station heard the call for back-up on their radio and arrived in time to capture the whole sordid scene on videotape. The officers that remained

moved in closer and cocked their guns. They were pissed-off that they were afraid and more than ready to share their hostile feelings with the creature in the coffin.

One of them yelled, "FREEZE—whatever the fuck you are, or I'll blow your head off!"

Terrified and confused, the Reverend raised his hands in the air. Clumps of gore dropped from his arms as he reached for the sky. The edgy officers mistook this universal sign of surrender for a threatening zombie pose. They jumped back. One of them squeezed off several rounds. His hands were shaking so hard that all the bullets missed their mark and ricocheted off the walls and ceiling of the mausoleum. Everyone dove for cover as the bullets zipped around the concrete crypt. Several officers jumped to their feet and approached the coffin. Upon closer inspection, they could see that the menacing monster was quite human after all. They slapped a pair of handcuffs on the revolting reverend and pulled him out of Courtney's coffin.

As the officers' fear subsided, a profound sense of disgust took its place. They winced and shook their heads as they surveyed the partially devoured corpses. One of the young female officers read the Reverend his rights. Her partner turned to the Reverend and said, "I'm not sure which laws you've broken pal, but I know you've broken a bunch of them."

The Reverend babbled incoherently, "Devil bitch . . . that spawn of Satan did this . . ."

As the police led the Reverend outside, one of the lady cops looked at him and said, "O.K., party boy, you've had enough fun for one night."

Margo watched as they stuffed Reverend Aldridge into a squad car and drove away. She slipped off silently across the cemetery and ran home.

It was two miles to the Woodbury compound. Margo ran hard and made it in fourteen minutes. When she got home,

she snuck in the kitchen door and crept up the back stairs to her room. Sweat poured off her as she stripped off her filthy clothes and jumped in the shower. The stinging stream of steaming water and fragrant, soapy lather seemed to wash away some of the horror. She dried off, crawled into bed and hoped her father hadn't noticed that she'd been gone. After a few minutes she heard heavy footsteps running up the stairs—then a knock on her door.

"Are you in there, Margo?" It was her father.

"Yes, Daddy." She feigned a sleepy voice.

"Come downstairs fast, you've got to see something!" her father yelled frantically as he ran back down stairs.

Margo slipped her robe on and walked calmly through the thick oak doorway of the study. She found her father gawking at the eleven o'clock news. The television flickered with a live broadcast from the Woodbury Mausoleum. The field reporter recounted the details of the bizarre event that occurred 45 minutes earlier. The anchor grimaced with every grizzly revelation. Margo's father held his head as the story unfolded. He was in a mild state of shock as they showed Courtney and Chad's violated remains.

Margo pretended to be equally horrified, "Who would do such a horrible thing?"

"They have Reverend Aldridge in custody, honey. I can't believe he could have done this, but they say they're going to show a tape of the arrest." Woodbury nervously ran his fingers through his thick silver hair.

Margo's butt started to itch again. Without thinking, she reached back and scratched her crack with a vengeance.

Her Father looked up and scolded, "Margo! Stop that—That's no way for a lady to behave."

"Sorry, Daddy," Margo stopped and covertly pressed her inflamed anus against the cool, smooth arm of a green leather chair.

The anchor announced that they were about to "roll the tape." The screen erupted with the gruesome scene inside the mausoleum. The jittery cameraman's shaky hand-held camera work added a strange sense urgency to the Reverend's bizarre arrest. Sure enough, there he was—big as life. The announcer called him the "Graveyard Ghoul." Margo bit her lip to keep from laughing. Her father covered his eyes and shook his head. He peeked through his parted fingers as they showed gory close-ups of the mangled corpses. Charles couldn't take it anymore. He moaned and turned the set off.

Margo and her father sat quietly in the dimly lit den. Margo stared into the popping fire while her father pinched the bridge of his nose with his thumb and forefinger.

After a long silence, Margo sighed and said, "Daddy?"

"What, honey?" His voice sounded dazed and distant.

"If I die before you, will you do me a favor?"

He glanced at her with a pained expression, "Sure, honey. What is it?"

"If I die before you, would you please have me cremated?"

He paused for a moment and replied, "If that's what you really want—sure."

He watched her pick a stringy piece of something gray and rubbery from between her teeth and toss it into the fire.

Then he said, "Oh, by the way, I didn't see you at dinner this evening—where did you run off to after the funeral?"

Margo thought for a moment, shifted her itchy ass in her chair and answered, "I ran into some relatives I hadn't seen for awhile at the cemetery. I went to their place and had a *yummy* family dinner."

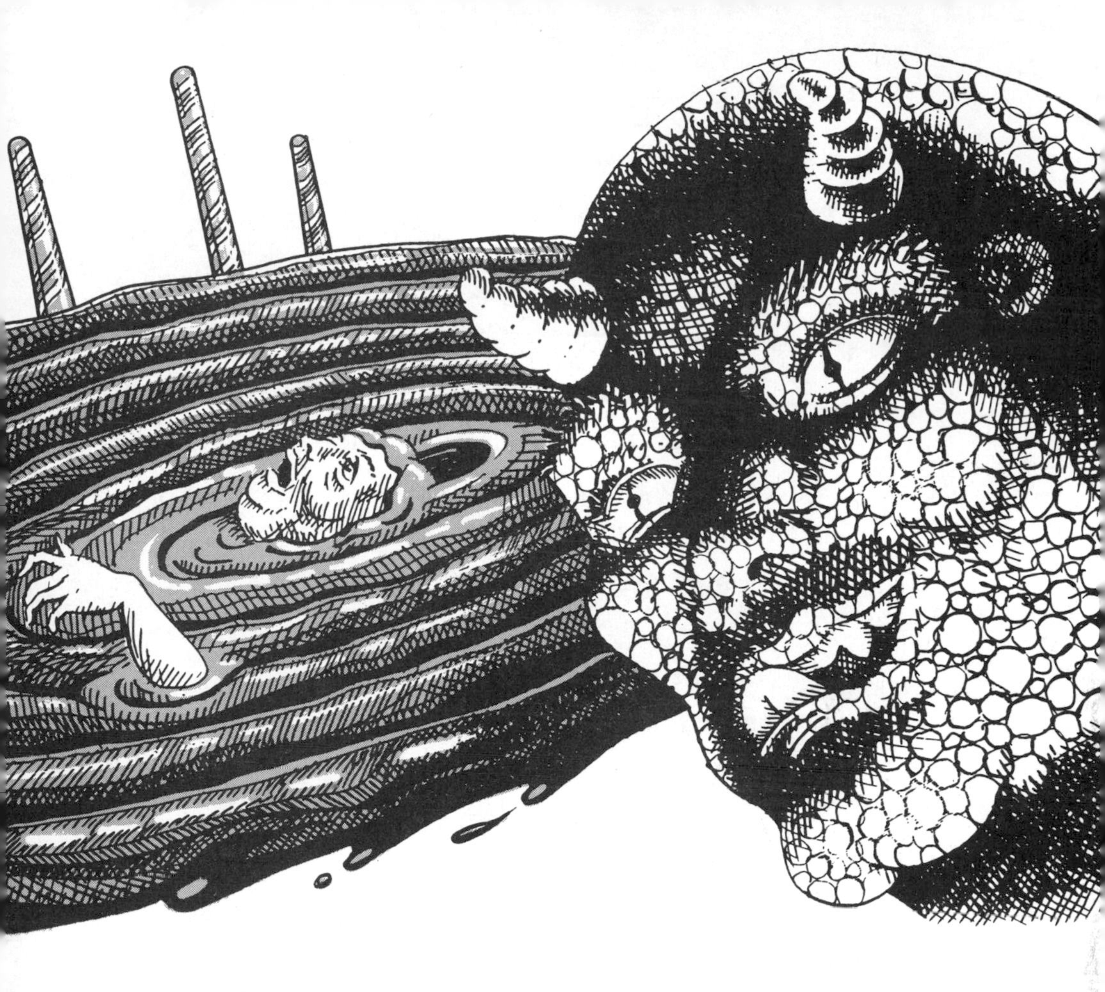

Tainted Treats

Before I went to bed last night,
I ate a rich dessert.
I stuffed myself with devil's food
Until my belly hurt.

As restless slumber numbs my pain,
I dream of tainted treats.
Barbaric boogy bakermen
Torment me with their sweets.

The Fiend of Fudge is one of them.
  He's fierce and foul and fat—
An edgy and aggressive man
  Who wears a small white hat.

He chases me down frosting lanes;
  I'm stuck in sticky goo.
He says, "Don't squirm! If you relax,
  I have a treat for you."

A horde of his assistants bring
  A pot of boiling fudge;
They have a long red rubber tube.
  I'm trapped, I can not budge.

They stick one end into the fudge—
  The other up my butt.
I get a hot fudge enema—
  It burns inside my gut.

They laugh and fall down on the ground,
  I cry and run away;
And as I do the fudge plops out.
  Then I hear someone say,

"Slow down my lovely farting friend
  And taste my sweet surprise.
I am The Candy Eyeball Man.
  Please try my candied eyes."

He's tall and cruel and sinister,
With taut and sallow skin.
He pries my mute mouth open wide
And pops an eyeball in.

The eye is soft and slippery
And has a chocolate glaze.
It leaves a loathsome aftertaste,
Like rancid mayonnaise.

He grabs my jaw and jams it shut.
The eye pops in my teeth.
The jiggling gel engulfs my tongue,
Above and underneath.

I struggle as I gasp and choke,
Eyes quiver in the bowl.
He scoops a heaping handful up
And makes me eat it whole.

I gag and heave the candy eyes.
They splatter on the floor.
He says, "There's more where those came from."
I stumble out his door.

I stagger down a narrow street
Of pastel marzipan,
Then stroll a pastry promenade
And try to form a plan.

The bakeries have all been made
With gingerbread and jam
And trimmed with frosted filagree.
I don't know where I am.

A man whose head is wide and round
Calls from a doughnut shop,
"My name is Mister Sinker, dear—
You're safe with me, please stop."

His forehead has a big round hole;
And yet he seems quite nice.
His doughnuts look so good to me,
I ask about the price.

"They are a lot of dough," he says,
Then laughs at his own joke,
"Your nightshirt has no pockets dear—
It looks like you are broke."

He shouts, "Your money's no good here!
The doughnuts are on me.
For hungry sleepyheads like you
My treats are always free."

His doughnuts look so sweet and fresh,
It's difficult to choose.
He shows me one that's jelly filled
And I can not refuse.

It's hot and fresh and smells so good,
  I take a greedy bite.
I munch away in mindless bliss,
  Then freeze in sudden fright.

There's something moving in my mouth—
  The thing falls from my hand.
I spit a mangled mouthful out.
  I feel too weak to stand.

I barf and fall down to my knees;
  And then I take a dive
Into the putrid pool of puke—
  The vomit is alive!

A mass of insects crawl and creep—
  They're squirming in the stuff.
Then Mister Sinker says to me,
  "I think you've had enough."

The center of the doughnut teems
  With maggots, ants and slugs.
I jump back from the moving mass
  Of jelly, barf and bugs.

I run from Mister Sinker's shop.
  He smiles and waves goodbye.
I can't believe he makes those things,
  He's such a friendly guy.

I scale a mincemeat mountain range;
  Then swim a pudding sea.
I walk down rancid rocky-road;
  And climb a gumball tree.

In twilight's jaundiced glow I spy
  The Land of Creepy Cake.
It's molding there in gray-green fuzz
  Beside a syrup lake.

I see a man with stubby horns;
  His broad and brutish shape
Stands out in frightening silhouette,
  Against the sweet landscape.

He stands before a mixing bowl
  That's big beyond belief.
Beside it, people stand in line.
  They moan and wail with grief.

They're cold and fat and naked.
  They cry and shake with fear.
He glares at me with fiendish glee
  And yells, "Get over here!"

I hesitate and look around.
  He roars, "Yea, I mean you!"
I slowly walk toward the beast
  And wonder what to do.

He holds the line and grabs my arm
And yanks me to the front.
He laughs and looks me up and down,
Then greets me with a grunt.

He's red and rude and menacing.
He snaps his pointed tail
And pokes his finger in my ribs.
I feel his fingernail.

He blows a snot-wad out his nose.
It splatters on my cheek.
I wipe it off and start to shake
As he begins to speak,

"I am the demon, Devil's Food.
Strip down and get in line.
My cake needs someone sweet like you.
I know you'll taste divine."

He flips me with his sharp pitchfork,
I fly into the bowl.
His bubbling batter swallows me.
I spin and toss and roll.

Huge metal blades spin fast and hard.
I flip head over heels.
The poor souls in his recipe
Cry out in desperate squeals.

The sharp blades slash a screaming man
 And split the guy in half.
They slice again and then again—
 The demon starts to laugh.

I feel the crunch of bone on bone
 As heads and limbs collide.
The mangled mulch of body parts
 Is tossed from side to side.

A dark brown blob pops up above
 The surface of the fudge.
Two pleading eyes stare straight at me,
 Then sink beneath the sludge.

I cry, "How did I get in here?"
 The demon-chef replies,
"It has to do with gluttony
 And how a person dies."

"In your case, you ate too much cake
  Before you went to bed.
Your heart stopped while you were asleep
  And now my dear, you're dead."

I shriek and spin around the bowl,
  Toward the slashing blade.
But as I tumble to my fate
  My dream begins to fade.

I wake up screaming in the night;
  Wrapped up in cold wet sheets.
I think that for the next few days
  I'll stay away from sweets.

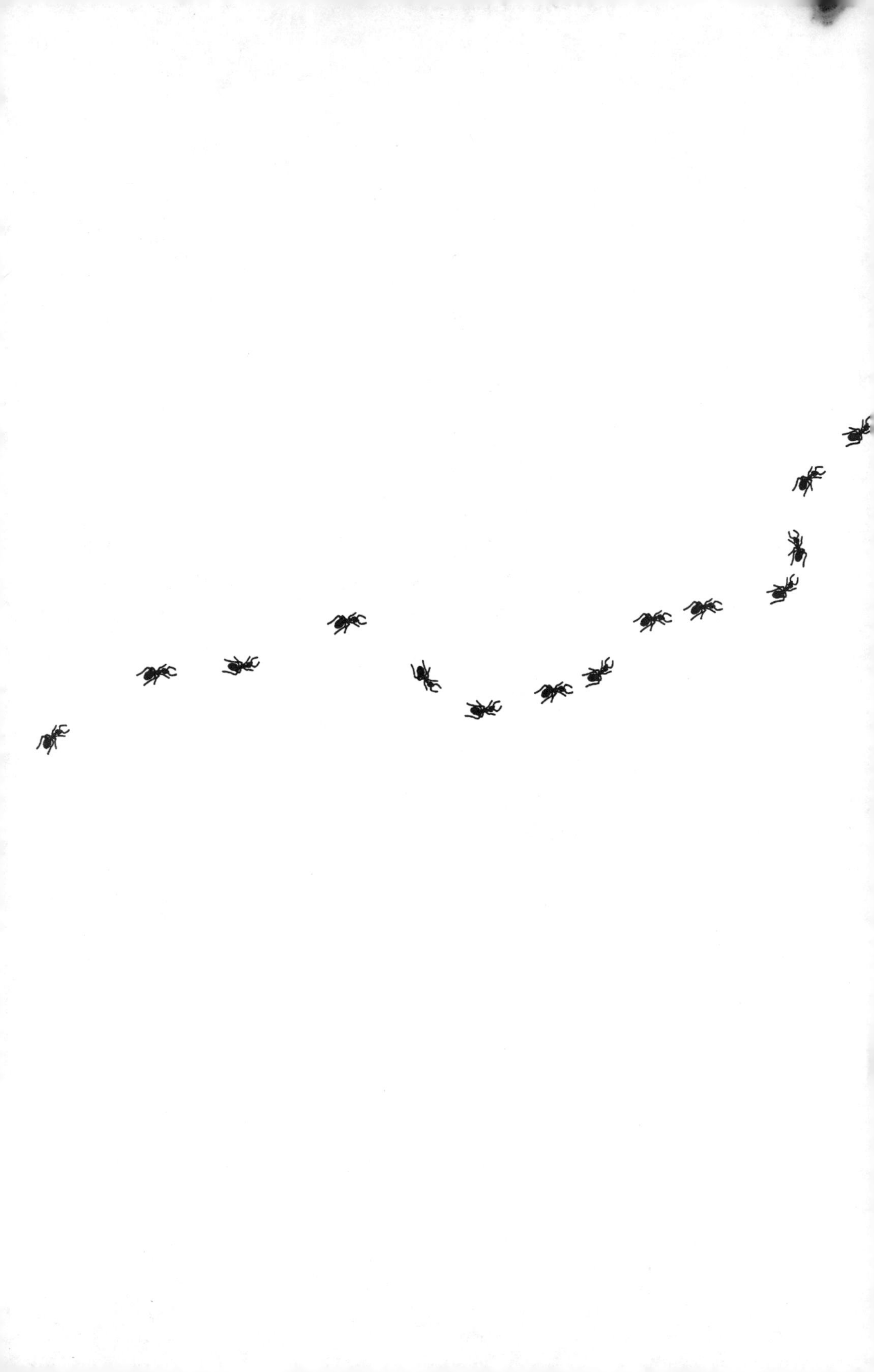